Eko & Indra
The Summer Olympians

Roger Schafer

Dedication

This story is dedicated to my family: to my mother, Barbara Schafer, my father, Roger Schafer, and my brothers, Michael and Danny Schafer.

I also would like to thank everyone involved in this project and hope you all enjoy the next adventures of Eko and Indra.

Acknowledgment

A lot of people believe that there is nothing you can do alone, and you always need the support of someone else around you to help you achieve something. Similar is the case with me. I have a lot of people who played a part in assisting me with the completion of this book and with this section I would like to extend my gratitude towards them.

About the Author

Roger *"Derby"* Schafer was born in New Mexico and has lived in Las Vegas, Nevada, most of his adult life. In the past, he played and coached numerous sports. As a Coach in Roller Hockey, his Team Won Nationals once and often had top teams competing on National Level for many years. He is the oldest of the three children in his family, all who reside in Las Vegas, Nevada.

Preface
A Quick Recap

The story of Eko and Indra picks up a few weeks after the exciting events of *The Perfect Season* when the Suparman brothers had their first perfect baseball season. They upheld their undefeated streak in both the regular season and the World Series Playoffs for the Albuquerque Conquistadors' first season.

The older of the identical twins, Eko translates to the *"Oldest One,"* while Indra literally means *"The Strong One."* Now twenty years of age, each standing 8 feet 8 inches tall, the Suparman brothers are as close to supermen as you can get. Both have running speeds that are faster than racecars, and that's no exaggeration – they're capable of running 364 miles per hour. They possess levels of strength and endurance never seen in the world before.

It has been less than a year since the world was introduced to Eko and Indra through an *"accident."* Prior to that, they were completely unknown, and now they are the two most recognized and most popular faces around the world. They have begun to change the world for the better, and are currently revolutionizing sports like baseball, which has now become more modern thanks to their capabilities directly influencing both technology and officiating. With the 2032 Summer Olympics soon approaching, Eko and Indra get ready to embark on their next set of adventures!

Contents

Page Left Blank Intentionally

Chapter 1
Life after 'The Perfect Season'

It has been nearly 6 weeks since Eko and Indra's last adventures, and since they, along with members of their original tribe, found a new location to call home in Australia. Eko Suparman is now engaged to Susan, and Indra Suparman is engaged to Aspyn. Roger is now retired from baseball. Sheldon's best friend and top advisor, Barbara Sue, and security and bodyguards Michael Dean and Daniel Joe live here too, along with the rest of the original tribe members.

Today is a special day for everyone. The entire village is waiting for the arrival of the owner of the Albuquerque Conquistadors Sheldon Winn, General Manager of the Conquistadors Bill Bell, Ronald Levi, the Tech Guru, and the President of Indonesia. This is the biggest day of Eko and Indra's life. For this is the day that Eko marries his fiancée Susan Vallelunga and Indra marries his fiancée Aspyn Walling, both together. After all, brothers have always done everything together, and it makes sense they'd both get married to the women they love on the same day too!

As Sheldon and the other guests finally arrive, they are greeted uproariously by all the villagers. Everyone is excited about the big wedding today, celebrating and eager for it to begin. A wedding is a very important event in Indonesian culture - it is considered to be the starting point of a new aspect of a person's life. And so, everyone wants to be part of the celebration. Literally, every person you know, from relatives to colleagues to business partners to mere acquaintances, could be an eligible invitee.

On the occasion of Eko and Indra's weddings, the brothers had invited basically everyone they had ever met and worked with since their journey started. Because of their worldwide fame, both of them are extremely popular with people all over the world and have a lot of people in attendance. Indonesians are truly honored by your attendance at a wedding.

Attending shows that you care, that you respect the people involved and your relationship with them, and that you honor the family and want to show your support of the newlyweds. Indonesian weddings involve a lot of ceremonies. There is the Akad Nikah, which is the actual wedding ceremony, and then there are Javanese customs as well as the Resepsi Pernikahan – the wedding reception. All of these will be performed on the same day for Eko and

Susan, and for Indra and Aspyn, as they join each other in holy matrimony and begin their starting point. Everyone is dressed sharply for the event, gorgeous and appropriately long-sleeved dresses on the women and business suits, or a long-sleeved batik shirt with slacks for the men. Even Sheldon honored this tradition as did all the other men that were not of the village but there as honored guests.

It is not necessary for an expatriate woman to cover her head, though many of the Indonesian attendees may do so based on older traditions. Idah thoughts on this were summed up thus: *"Before moving to our new home here, we as a people were limited to what we wore. But one thing about our tradition remains the same – then and now, you, the guests, do as you wish, and dress as you desire, with no judgment from anyone."*

After all, all the people of the original tribe, along with Roger, Aspyn, and Susan, have become a part of the village and new tribe, where the extended family is home. Roger, Susan, and Aspyn have been with Eko and Indra since or even before Eko and Indra first entered the United States.

The home will be where the family is, not just a location. When the season was, and events in Indonesia were over, the whole world helped out. Plus, when these events first started, Sheldon asked Barbara Sue, his oldest, best and most trusted friend, to join Eko and Indra to take care of them. Barbara was more than happy to oblige. She, too, is part of this large family.

The bride and groom may customarily be preceded by traditional dancers who perform before the wedding couples go on stage. Or the performance may take place after the bride and groom are seated. However, Eko and Indra decided to have traditional dances both before and after, so all of the villagers could be involved on this special day.

A special dance was chosen that depicted everyone attending. Even the security would do a performance before the wedding. The dance showed a wonderfully constructed tale of the events that started back on the Island that was home and continued to tell of Roger and his parachute, Eko, Indra, and Idah's trip to the USA, Eko, and Indra's baseball games, as well as their travel stories. It was a performance to treasure, more of a show than dance and both truthful and funny.

The parents of the bride and groom and other senior family members are then supposed to follow the couples in procession into the room. Eko and Indra had Idah and

Roger stand in for their deceased parents. Since Eko was the older twin, he and Susan were followed by Indra and Aspyn. Their senior family members included their uncle and his wife, followed by Sheldon and Barbara. Susan's parents were next, and then Aspyn's parents, and then 20 more men and 17 more women from Eko and Indra's tribe.

Then come the speeches! A representative of each family will address the crowd to thank them for their attendance and sometimes express regret if any of the arrangements for the reception are lacking or found wanting. Depending on whether or not you have one or two representatives speak, the speeches can be very brief or take up to half an hour or longer.

The first to speak was Idah. She reminded the audience how she found the boys awash on the shore from what was indeed a verified and confirmed shipwreck. The father of Eko and Indra was a grief-stricken widower who had lost his wife very recently. He had been trying to give his sons a better life. The man made sure his two infant sons were safe and sacrificed his own life to allow them a chance to survive, which they both did.

"The boys weren't crying, but I could hear the sounds of babies gurgling, so I ran down to the beach and found

5

them. All they had on was bracelets on their wrists – one saying Eko Suparman and the other Indra Suparman. That's how I knew their family name. Roger followed Idah. His speech told everyone about the events that happened and how Eko and Indra helped make a better world. He spoke of the many events involving Eko and Indra that continued to improve millions of lives worldwide.

Sheldon came on now. He talked about how all sports now have changed for the better, thanks to Eko and Indra. *"They changed our world and made it a better place. There are now so many jobs and benefits all over the world, all because of Eko and Indra. Roger is right; the biggest thing that Eko and Indra have done and continue to do is improve our planet."*

It was Ron's turn after Sheldon, and he started by saying, "Sheldon is right. You see, if we didn't know about Eko and Indra or have them around, all sports would still be as they used to be. We have completely changed and modernized everything, and that was only because of Eko and Indra. Eko and Indra have indeed made the world a better place for everyone: for babies, children, men, and women, and I am proud to know them."

Everyone had something to say, and none of it was bad or negative, except for how Eko and Indra's farts were by far the stinkiest, loudest, and longest of all the farts ever, especially when they would keep eating that American food. Many of the children vouched for the truth of this. Eko only blushes when he sees Susan as does Indra when he sees Aspyn. It was very rare that either of them would blush, but every time it was mentioned, they both did turn red. Because of their nature, they were not at all upset, but they were definitely embarrassed for it was indeed the truth. All the children giggled, as did many of the older guests.

After the speeches, the guests are invited to come to the stage and shake the hands of the bride and groom and their closest loved ones. These were Susan and Aspyn's parents, and Roger and Idah, for the twins. This part of the ceremony can go on for hours, depending on the number of guests in the receiving line. Yet, thankfully, it didn't take that long now, which was lucky because everyone was ready for some traditional Indonesian music and hungry for the wedding buffet. Since Susan and Aspyn were both American-born, the traditional Indonesian wedding was mixed with some aspects of an American wedding as well. The wedding, therefore, combined Western and Indonesian styles, a mixture of both cultures. Popular songs from both cultures played during this part of the celebration.

Yes, Aspyn and Susan do love their Top 40 and hip hop, as did most of the other villagers, since everyone in the village did speak many languages because of Idah. And the music was one of the things that expanded in scope for Eko and Indra, as well as everyone in the village. Eko and Indra enjoyed Bruno Mars, Lady Gaga, Beyonce, and many other popular singers.

The ceremony was spectacular and proceeded wonderfully. Everyone was having a great time, now that Eko and Susan Suparman, and Indra and Aspyn Suparman are now officially man and wife. After the festivals and celebrating are complete, it is time for each couple to seal the marriage that evening. The women split into two groups as evenly as possible.

The men do the same thing, splitting into two groups as evenly as they can. First to exit was Susan, who was then escorted by one of the groups of two women to her new home with Eko. Next to exit was Aspyn, and the remaining women escorted her to her new home with Indra. Now that the two married women had been delivered to their homes, all the women began to celebrate by dancing and singing.

Susan and Aspyn now waited for their husbands to be escorted to them.

Eko exited, and one of the two groups of men led him to where Susan was waiting. She was waiting outside, and as Eko arrived, he picked her up in his arms as they waited for Indra to be escorted to his wife and home. Indra arrived, led by the remaining group of men to his new home and his bride Aspyn. Indra saw how Eko was holding Susan and then picked up Aspyn before turning to face the crowd, where everyone - men, women, and children, were all celebrating with joy.

Both couples now stood at their front doors and waved to their guests to thank them and bid them goodbye. Next, Eko and Indra then carried their wives into their homes and closed the doors without locking them – none of the doors had any locks. The only lock was the security and bodyguards Michael Dean, and Daniel Joe "DJ" had locks for where they slept, because of having weapons. Yet, No one in the entire village had locks, except here.

All the guests remained at the site of the village. Later the next day, when Eko and Indra woke after their first night as married men, they gathered with the other men, as did Susan and Aspyn with the other women. All four of them were visibly glowing; one could see the love they brought to each other. Never had any of the villagers, or even Idah and Roger, ever seen Eko and Indra as happy as they were.

And everyone had seen Eko and Indra happy; after all, they were happy 99% of the time, and yet today, they noticeably appeared to be the happiest they had ever been. They were all congratulated again for the wedding and success of the marriage, and many people voiced their hope that new babies would be added to this village in the near future. The President of Indonesia arrived at the gathering, sitting between Eko and Indra.

Even though they are now in Australia and call this home, the Indonesian island they grew up in would always be their true home. So they gave the President ultimate respect, and the President returned the same respect to Eko, Indra, and all the other villagers and guests present. The President asked Eko and Indra how their night was. They responded with smiles and continued to glow in almost in a spiritual way.

It was indeed an excellent night for both of them, and as the rumors make the rounds around the tribe, it came to be known it had been a great night – at least, that was what

Susan and Aspyn were telling the other women in the village, who told the men of the tribe.

The President congratulated the two young men. Then he said, *"Eko and Indra, now you are married. You have been so successful, and represented all of us in Indonesia. Are you two ready to add another milestone to your careers? Are you ready to participate in the upcoming Summer Olympics in Russia in 2032?"*

Eko and Indra had, after all, told the President several weeks ago that they would be more than happy to represent Indonesia in the Upcoming 2032 Summer Olympics. They had been busy with the new home they recently set up, as well as with all the fundraisers and the meetings with different people all over the world to provide everyone with clean water, food, medical, school, and structured sports including baseball (because of Eko and Indra, baseball was now the most played sport in the world.)

So at this point, it would not only be an honor but would also give Eko and Indra a chance to compete in a wide variety of events that would challenge them, as they had never been tested as Olympians. After all, the Olympics are the first and original sporting event. It is truly a worldwide competition where Eko and Indra should be very successful and have a huge impact, perhaps even bigger than what they had done for baseball.

Sheldon frowned. He was not too happy about this since it would mean interference and conflicts for the upcoming Conquistadors Baseball Season. Sheldon was very aware that without the Twin Suparmans on his team, they would have a poor chance of defending their World Series. His hopes of duplicating that first-ever and only perfect season in all categories of all seasonal stats would all be shattered. Any kind of repeat would have to involve Eko and Indra maintaining the same levels of last season's game mastery that they had displayed.

At 20, the twins were not at an age when most experts believe the best is yet to come in terms of what they could do, as they continued to mature and grow older, stronger, and wiser. Many believed Eko and Indra had still not reached their peak, and that they would be even better as they grow older. Roger responded to the President's statement. "Eko and Indra are now grown married men," he said. "I think that they should do that which they want, regardless of what others may think. After all, they have earned that right."

Of course, Sheldon was not happy at hearing this, either. Rather than say anything, however, he stood up, nodded his head as if in approval, and began to make his way to where Idah and Barbara were sitting.

Idah and Barbara noticed that Sheldon was walking towards the group of women. Both of them knew Sheldon well enough to know that something was troubling him. Idah and Barbara each stood up and started walking in the direction of Sheldon. "Sheldon, what is wrong?" asked Idah as they reached him. Sheldon told both women about how they, Eko and Indra would be representing Indonesia in the Summer Olympics in Russia next summer, at the same time as the Conquistadors baseball games, knowing that they would miss all or most of those baseball games during the Summer Olympics.

"Sheldon, what is wrong with that?" said Barbara. "They made a promise, and they have delivered you not just a World Series, but also have given you and the Conquistadors the first-ever perfect season too."

Sheldon dropped his head upon hearing this. After all, he above anyone knows what Eko and Indra have done for him, both professionally and personally. It was because of the brothers that Sheldon was now the world's richest person, and the first-ever trillionaire – and it wasn't just one trillion anymore; it was growing by the second.

Idah smiled. "Sheldon, do not worry. They are young right now, but both Eko and Indra love you and do not want to bring you any bad news. They do not want to make you upset or sad."

"Yes, I know," said Sheldon. "You're both right. It just caught me off-guard. But I do understand, and I know a thing about making promises and keeping them."

Barbara knew this to be true and gave Sheldon a smile before hugging him, for he was indeed Barbara's best friend.

Sheldon then said: "I will accept what they wish to do. However, as the Owner of the team and with everything happening, Barbara, I have a request of you. Would you mind continuing to stay with Eko and Indra and help them, along with Aspyn and Susan?"

Idah jumped at this. "Yes, please, Barbara! Please stay, for soon we are to have new babies, and we can use all the help."

Barbara was more than happy, for she had found comfort, something which had touched her since she had been with the villagers after they all left the USA. In many ways, this was Barbara's family now as well, and her friendship with Idah was nearly as strong as it was with Sheldon. She accepted Sheldon's request with a 100% desire to be a part of this community.

It was agreed that Barbara Sue would stay with the Idah to help the villagers, as well as Aspyn and Susan, in any way she could. Given that she was Sheldon's oldest and closest friend whom he trusted unlike anyone else, she was very capable of getting things done when needed or necessary, such as hiring Michael Dean and Daniel Joe, two of the best bodyguards in the world. Michael Dean and *"DJ,"* aka Daniel Joe, are intimidating even to look at, both of them standing at 6 feet 8 inches tall. However, they do not look at all intimidating when Eko or Indra are standing near them.

At any other time, however, they'll be the most intimidating people in the room. Plus, they are fierce, loyal, trained, capable, and intelligent. These two were on the United States Presidential Personal Detail until Sheldon hired them away to ensure Eko, Indra, Idah, and the other villagers would be safe from anyone who would potentially kidnap and use as hostage any one of the brothers' family, village and loved ones.

As the day was ending, Sheldon and the President of Indonesia prepared to leave together in the helicopter that would transport them to Sydney Airport so they could head back to their destinations: Sheldon to Albuquerque, New Mexico and the President to Jakarta, Indonesia. After all, work has to be done, and life doesn't stop. Much will need to be done immediately by both of these busy Men. When it was officially announced how Eko and Indra would be representing Indonesia in the 2032 Summer Olympic Russia Games, all of the other 35 baseball owners jumped with joy. Most of them are hoped Eko and Indra would take the entire season off; after all, they proved to be unstoppable and had yet to lose a baseball game.

Thus it was something the other professional baseball teams were happy to hear being *"OFFICIALLY ANNOUNCED."* Eko and Indra would indeed be in the 2032 Summer Olympics in Moscow, Russia. It was now official. The entire world knew.

ROGER SCHAFER

Chapter 2
Olympic Facts

The first Olympic Games date back to 775 B.C., originating in Athens, Greece, and is known for being the beginning of major sporting events as we know today. June 23rd, 1894 A.D. is the date the International Olympic Committee (IOC) was formed, the birth of the Modern Olympics. Since then, the IOC has been involved in every Olympic, both Summer and Winter, to this day.

The Olympics of 1896 are considered the Greatest Olympics ever. They were held in Athens, Greece, and all the events took place at the Panathinaiko Stadium, the biggest and first modern stadium at the time. At this time, the Olympics were held every 4 years, and the Winter Olympics had not been conceived of yet. Here's a look at the years and locations of the following Summer Olympics:

1896 Athens, Greece	1900 Paris, France	1904 St. Louis, USA
1908 London, England	1912 Stockholm, Sweden	1916 canceled due to WWI
1920 Antwerp, Belgium	1924 Paris, France	1928 Amsterdam, Netherlands
1932 Los Angeles,	1936 Belin,	1940 relocated to

USA	German	Helsinki, Finland
1944 canceled due to WWII	1952 Helsinki, Finland	1956 Melbourne, Australia
1960 Rome, Italy	1964 Tokyo, Japan	1968 Mexico City, Mexico
1972 Munich, Germany	1976 Montreal, Canada	1980 Moscow, Russia
1984 Los Angeles, USA	1988 Seoul, Korea	1992 Barcelona, Spain
1996 Atlanta, USA	2000 Sydney, Australia	2004 Athens, Greece
2008 Beijing, China	2012 London, England	2016 Rio De Janeiro, Brazil
2020 Tokyo, Japan	2024 Paris, France	2028 Los Angeles, USA
2032 Moscow, Russia*		

*The 2032 Summer Olympics are to be held next, later this year, in Moscow, Russia. The current record for the most gold medals won by any country was during 1984 during the Summer Olympics held in Los Angeles, USA Summer Olympics. The United States of America won 83 gold medals during those Summer Olympics, and now that Eko and Indra are competing for Indonesia in the 2032 Summer Olympics, this record may soon fall.

Early Olympic games were celebrated as a religious festival from 776 B.C. until 393 A.D. when the games were banned for being a pagan festival (the Olympics celebrated the Greek god Zeus). In 1894, a French educator, Baron Pierre de Coubertin, proposed a revival of the ancient tradition, and thus the modern-day Olympic Summer Games were born, and later, the International Olympic Committee. At the first Olympic Summer Games in 1896, the host country Greece won the most medals (47). The first Winter Olympic Games were held in Chamonix, France in 1924. The United States has won more medals at the Summer Games than any other country.

The five Olympic rings represent the five major regions of the world – Africa, the Americas, Asia, Europe, and Oceana. Every national flag in the world includes one of the five colors, which are (from left to right) blue, yellow, black, green, and red. Up until 1994, the Olympics were held every four years, both the Winter and Summer Olympics combined in one event. Since then, the Winter and Summer games have alternated every two years. The first televised Olympics were the 1960 Summer Games in Rome by CBS television from the United States of America.

No country in the Southern Hemisphere has ever hosted a Winter Games. Two continents – Africa and Antarctica – have never hosted an Olympics. A record of 212 countries participated in the 2028 Olympic Summer Games in Los Angeles.

The Summer Olympic sports usually include archery, badminton, basketball, beach volleyball, boxing, canoe/kayak, cycling, diving, equestrian, fencing, field hockey, gymnastics, handball, judo, modern pentathlon (shooting, fencing, swimming, show jumping, and running), mountain biking, rowing, sailing, shooting, soccer, swimming, synchronized swimming, table tennis, taekwondo, tennis, track and field, triathlon (swimming, biking, running), volleyball, water polo, weightlifting, and wrestling.

Each host country also will have non-standard events and submit a variety of sports and possible events for Olympic Consideration, which normally would be allowed.

- The first Olympic Games took place in the 8th century B.C. in Olympia, Greece. They were held every four years for 12 centuries. Then, in the 4th century A.D., all pagan festivals were banned by

Emperor Theodosius; the Olympics and I were no more.

- The athletic tradition was resurrected about 1500 years later. The first modern Olympics were held in 1896 in Greece and have continued since then. The Olympics have only ever been canceled due to major world wars.

- In ancient Greece, athletes didn't worry about sponsorship, protection, or fashion – they competed naked. During modern times, it has not been allowed to compete naked.

- Back then, the games lasted five or six months.

- Women have been allowed to compete in the Olympics since 1900.

- From 1924-1992, the Winter and the Summer Olympics took place in the same year. Now, they're on separate cycles and alternate every two years.

- Only seven athletes have won medals in both the Winter and the Summer Olympics. Only one of them, Christa Ludinger-Rothenburger, won medals in the same year.

- During the 2012 London Games, the Olympic village required 165,000 towels for more than two weeks of activity.

- The official languages of the games are English and French, complemented by the official language of the host country. This year it will include Russian since Russia is hosting the Summer Olympics.

- Tarzan competed in the Olympics: Johnny Weissmuller, an athlete-turned-actor who played Tarzan in 12 movies, won five gold medals in swimming in the 1920s.

- From 1912-1948, artists participated in the Olympics: painters, sculptors, architects, writers, and musicians competed for medals in their respective fields.

- During the 1936 Berlin Games, two Japanese pole-vaulters tied for second place. Instead of competing again, they cut the silver and bronze medals in half and fused the two different halves together so that each of them had a half-silver and half-bronze medal.

- The Olympic torch is lit the old-fashioned way in an ancient ceremony at the temple of Hera in Greece:

Actresses, wearing costumes of Greek priestesses, use a parabolic mirror and sun rays for kindling the torch.

- From there, the torch starts its relay to the host city: It is usually carried by runners, but it has traveled on a boat, on an airplane (and the Concorde), on horseback, on the back of a camel, via radio signal, underwater, and in a canoe.

- The unlit Olympic torch has also been taken to space several times.

- The relay torch and the Olympic flame are supposed to burn during the whole event. In case the flame goes out, it can only be reignited with a backup flame, which has been lit in Greece as well. Never has a regular lighter been used; only the original torch or back up torch will light the fire!

- The 2012 London Games were the first Olympics in which all participating countries sent female athletes.

- The following sports are (sadly) not part of the Olympics anymore: solo synchronized swimming, tug of war, rope climbing, hot air ballooning, dueling pistol, tandem bicycle, swimming obstacle race, and plunge for distance. Luckily, live pigeon shooting was a one-shot and only part of the 1900 Olympics in Paris.

- The five rings of the Olympic symbol – designed by Baron Pierre de Coubertin, co-founder of the modern Olympic Games – represent the five inhabited continents of the world.

- The six colors – blue, yellow, black, green, red, and the white background – were chosen because every nation's flag contains at least one of them.

- The Olympic Games have been hosted by 25 different countries.

- The first official Olympic mascot was Waldi, the dachshund, at the 1972 Games in Munich.

- The 2016 Games in Rio is the first time the Olympics are held in South America.

- During the 17 days of the 2016 Summer Olympics, 10,500 athletes from 205 countries will represent 42 different sports and participate in 306 competitions in Rio.

- The 2032 Summer Games will make use of the greatest and most advanced scoring and judging systems the world has ever seen.

Because of Eko and Indra, the OIC will now have to work with Ronald Levi to have up and running timekeepers, scoring systems, anything everything related to both contestants and fans' safety. The games will be modernized as baseball was, for both correct and proper scoring. They will also need to be updated to keep fans, and other competitors safe from the effects of the feats Eko and Indra are capable of.

The Summer Games 2032 became official once the OIC ensured the use of advanced technology designed by Ronald Levi so Eko and Indra could compete. Now that the Suparman twins are becoming Olympians, it will be interesting to see how many new Olympian Records will be set in the upcoming Summer Olympics in Moscow, Russia, and how many of them will break the current World Records.

Chapter 3
2032 Summer Olympic Events

The scheduled events for the 2032 Summer Olympics have been established, with 165 different men's events and 20 different mixed (men/women). The most difficult task will be to find out which events Eko and Indra can participate in. They will not be in any event that requires a gun, for they have never had or even shot a gun. Any events that are gun-related are automatically disqualified for consideration by Eko and Indra.

This year's Olympics will last a total of 19 days, which includes some qualifying rounds. The Official 2032 Olympics, including the qualifying rounds, will begin on Wednesday, July 21, 2032, and run until Sunday, August 9th, 2032, which will be the last and final day of the 2032 Summer Olympics.

When it was first announced that Eko and Indra Suparman, also known as the *"Supermen Twins,"* was to compete in the Summer Olympics in Moscow, Russia, the IOC's "main office was flooded with non-stop calls. Any and all tickets that were not sold prior to the announcement for different Men and Mixed Olympic Events were sold within a matter of moments at the Russian Olympic Committee's ticket sales. During what is now known as the *"Perfect Season,"* the Suparmen Twins have become the highest profiled, most popular, and most globally followed athletes. There isn't a place anywhere, even in the remotest of locations that do not know of Eko and Indra in today's world. It's a dramatic change from just a year ago when no one knew either of them, with the exception of a small remote village with fewer than 75 people.

Now Eko and Indra will be able to give other people in different parts of the world the opportunity to see them in person. They will be performing in events they have little experience or knowledge of, with the exception of baseball, football, and basketball. After all, they did have a charity event for football (soccer) and basketball at the end of the baseball season.

Yes, they did win the World Baseball Championship, and in doing so, they became the one and only professional baseball team in any era to go undefeated all through the regular season and during the extended play-off. They broke every single season's record both offensively and defensively. Eko and Indra then took on the world's best football players (soccer) from all over the world and won that event. The case was the same when they played against the world's greatest basketball players. The biggest question prior to the Olympics is: will they lose? Can they compete in events they've never participated in? Will it be too much or too many events? How will they hold up? The media, as usual, is trying to find a way to make this a negative story, and coming up with many narratives, many of them completely false or negative.

After all, since no one actually knows all the facts, the media used the darker side of the picture to create sales or to increase the number of viewers/followers. They're focusing on the fact that any loss in any competition would be a first, not counting when Eko and Indra played with the village children. Those are the only times they lost any competition, while they would play with the children of their village or other children around the world.

They'd often play these games and lose to the children. The OIC and also Russian representatives were all very happy and excited about Eko and Indra's announcement of participation in the upcoming Summer Games. Just their involvement would ensure an extremely successful Olympics, and also would probably break all broadcast and attendance records. All of the hotels in and near Moscow were sold out. If you didn't have a room booked, you were not going to find a room to stay.

If you were a resident of Moscow with homes or a place to take on visitors, your space would be booked, rented out and paid for in full months in advance of the Games. Now that that was taken care of, it was time to update and modernize all the scoring, officiating, judging changes and requirements. Rooms were sold out before the games even started for the workers to make the necessary changes.

Because of Eko and Indra, they will need to improve all areas of officiating and also install safety netting to ensure that all fans will be safe, particularly for events like javelin, shot put, and hammer throws. They also need to make necessary changes required to ensure that all officiating is fair for all the athletes and events. Ronald Levi has been very busy in his efforts to make sure everything is ready for the pre-qualifying, qualifying and actual Olympic Events.

Sheldon is very happy, for this will ensure that his wealth grows even larger and keeps him in the position of the only trillionaire in the world at this time. Never in modern history has past Olympic Games, Summer or Winter, generated such a level of excitement and modern media buzz now. Because of Eko and Indra, you could flip the channels and see all the media updates, talk shows, and news featuring Eko and Indra, the soon-to-be Olympians.

It has been nearly two months since it was announced that Eko and Indra would be in the upcoming Summer Olympics. The IOC, Russians, and members of the Indonesian Official Olympic representatives were all meeting. These different groups are all busily ensuring scheduling, so everything would go smoothly without any conflicting issues. Many changes were made, so Eko, Indra, or both could participate in the events they wanted, too, hopefully without scheduling conflicts.

Not only are all the events being modernized to ensure the correct call and fairness for everyone, but safety is a paramount consideration for all those in attendance and near where the events will take place. These precautions are to be made for the pre-qualifying and qualifying events which will be held all over the world.

All three of the committee's – the IOC, the Russians, and the Indonesians wanted to make sure that as many of the upcoming events as possible would be available for both Eko and Indra, during any and all of the pre-qualifying, qualifying and finals of a wide variety of Olympic Events: the next step to make it to the Summer Olympics. After all the endless nights and long days of working together, they were able to make a schedule that would allow either Eko or Indra, and in some cases both Eko and Indra to compete in as many events as possible. When that was announced, people were excited at the thought: *"Are Eko and Indra going to compete against each other in some events?"* For that, it would be worth the price of admission to see Eko versus Indra.

What only a handful of people knew was that Eko and Indra would never compete directly against the other in the same event in front of an audience or any type of live competitive event, especially in something like boxing or UFC. Yet in some of the sporting events that involve weight classes, like wrestling, Greco-wrestling, judo, boxing, and weightlifting, Eko and Indra could compete in their actual weight class, and the other twin brother could move up a weight class to a higher level.

That way, they each could possibly win a gold medal in the exact same sport, except in different weight classes. And if it turned out to be legal, they have even more options at higher weight levels available. If the IOC approved it, they might compete in several different weight classes – for instance, boxing, wrestling or weightlifting. After all, it is the President of Indonesia's intention to break that all-time single Olympic Year Gold Medal set by the United States of America back in the Summer Olympics 1984 of 83 combined gold medals.

That was in itself the one and only goal that the President of Indonesia wanted and asked Eko and Indra to achieve - 84 gold medals or more, at this time. Sponsorship money was flowing into the Indonesian Olympic funds unlike ever before from both private and corporate sponsors. This was thanks to recent events creating friendships with Mr. Phillip Knight of Nike, Mr. Bill Gates, Mr. Sheldon Winn, and others during the time spent to improve the lives of millions of people all over the world. Now the Indonesian Olympians would compete with the other Giant 3: the United States of America, Russia, and the Chinese Olympic Teams.

Even as all of these events have been happening, Eko and Indra have never been happier than anytime they can recall. For both of their wives, Susan and Aspyn are both very much pregnant. Barbara has made sure that both women have been receiving the very best prenatal care and doctors possible. What was amazing was when it was found out that both Aspyn and Susan were confirmed to be pregnant with a set of twins each. The Amazing Twins, The Suparmen, Eko and Indra, were now both soon to be fathers, and both to twins! Yet for various reasons, including safety, Barbara and Idah have convinced everyone involved to keep this very low profile. They have done this with both sets of parent's approval and blessings.

The only people aware of this are the ones in the village, Sheldon, and the private doctors hired. After all, life at the village in Australia was peaceful and had absolutely zero crime or anything to worry about, just as it was in the home they lived for many years. The villagers didn't even have locks on any of the doors; even the bathrooms do not have locks.

The last thing the village wanted was to have the media, press, and television reporters knowing and then hundreds, thousands, or even hundreds of thousands of reporters, fans, visitors, or even potential threats to show up at their doorstep. This was something they learned from experience, from the time they were back in Indonesia where home used to be. They had also discovered this outside Santa Fe, New Mexico.

When the media others know about such happenings, they would lose all privacy, and it would also be made possible for those that would harm or hold them hostage to do something bad. This decision afforded Eko and Indra complete peace of mind. It also allowed them time to learn new skills, train, and practice for the events which they did not understand or have experience of yet. They also learned the rules, etiquette and other information they were not familiar with for the upcoming Summer Olympics in Russia.

Barbara, with Sheldon's blessing, ensured that Eko or Indra had everything they needed to learn and train for the various events that they would be taking on. Ron would, at times, also send items that helped review what they were doing and make suggestions on how to improve. And of course, Sheldon was always concerned about the health of Aspyn, Susan, and all four of the unborn children.

By this time, baseball season had started. A year ago at this time, they would have been in either in Albuquerque playing for the Conquistadors or on the road, playing a series against another professional baseball team. The happiest of the baseball people were all the other 35 team owners who knew that this year, without Eko and Indra, they had a chance to win this year's World Series.

Of course, the one owner that wasn't at all happy about all of this was Sheldon Winn. But Sheldon knew that all he could do was be supportive because after all, because of Eko and Indra, he had become the first-ever trillionaire in the word. His expansion team, the Conquistadors, had won every game and set every record in baseball, and most of that was because of Eko and Indra.

Chapter 4
2032 Olympic Events

The committees had spent nearly two months working and re-working the men's and mixed schedules. This included all pre-qualifying and qualifying events, as well as the finals. The IOC, the Russians, and the Indonesians were all able to complete a final list of events that Eko and Indra would be participating in for Indonesia.

The name of the event will be listed first, followed by either X1 or X2. The X1 will mean either Eko or Indra will be competing. The X2 means that both will compete if weight classes are involved, such as weight lifting, wrestling, or boxing. One will be in their actual weight class, and the other twin brother would move up a weight class and compete at the higher weight class. This was something that the General Public was hoping did not happen. Many in the media and also many fans worldwide were hoping, even praying, to have a final match of brother versus brother as an example. Yet, that wasn't going to happen, at least not in these 2032 Summer Olympics. Thus, any conflicts in the schedule are resolved.

The breakdowns are as follows:

Athletics/track and field (M is meters while K is kilometers.)

Archery X1

Track events:

100 M X1

200 M X1

400 M X1

800 M X1

1,500 M X1

5,000 M X1

10,000 M X1

Marathon X1

200 M relay X2

400 M relay X2

800 M relay X2

1,600 M relay X2

5,000 M relay X2

110 M Hurdles X1

400 M Hurdles X1

3,000 M Steeple Chase X1

4 X 100 M relay X2

4 X 400 M relay X2

20 K race walk X1

50 K race walk X1

High Jump X1

Pole Vault X1

Long Jump X1

Triple Jump X1

Shot Put X1

Hammer Throw X1

Discuss Throw X1

Javelin Throw X1

Decathlon X1

Eko and Indra will be competing in a total of 28 overall athletics/track and field events.

Badminton:
Singles X1

Doubles X2

Mixed Doubles X1

This will be a total of 3 events.

Basketball:
3 on 3 Basketball X1

Basketball 5 on 5 X1 or X2

Depending on the schedule, this will be 2 events.

Beach Volleyball X2

Boxing X2

Canoe:
200 M X1

1,000 M X1

This is a total of 4 Canoe events, two for "sprint and slalom."

Kayak:

200 M X1

2 person 200 M X1 or X2

1,000 M X1

2 person 1,000 M X1 or X2

4 man 1,000 M

This is 10 Kayak events, with a total of 5 each for "Spring and Slalom."

Cricket X1 or X2

Croquet X1 or X2

Cycling Road X1

Cycling Track X1

Diving:

SpringBoard Diving X1

Platform Diving X1

There are two diving events.

Fencing X1

Football X1 or X2*

Gymnastics:

Floor X1

Pommel Horse X1

Still Rings X1

Vault X1

Parallel Bars X1

Horizontal "High" Bar X1

There are six gymnastic events.

Handball X1 or X2

Field Hockey X1 or X2

Judo X2 (2 events for different weight classes)

Lacrosse X1 or X2

Marathon Swimming Open Water X1

Roller Hockey

3 on 3 Roller Hockey X1 or X2

4 on 4 Roller Hockey X1 or X2

Rowing

Single Scull X1

Double Scull X2

Quad Scull X2

Coxless Pairs X2

Coxless Pairs X2

Coxless fours X2

Coxed fours X2

Eights X2

This makes for 8 Rowing events, with the brothers using one oar each in the coxless   events.

Rugby X1 or X2

Swimming

100 M Backstroke X1	800 M Freestyle
100 M Breaststroke X1	1,000 M Backstroke X1
100 M Freestyle X1	1,000 M Breastroke X1
1,500 M Freestyle X1	1,000 M Freestyle X1
200 M Backstroke X1	200 M 4 man relay X1 or X2
200 M Breaststroke X1	
200 M Freestyle X1	400 M 4 man relay X1 or X2
400 M Backstroke X1	
400 M Breastroke X1	800 M 4 man relay X1 or X2
400 M Freestyle X1	
800 M Backstroke X1	1,000 M 4 man relay X1 or X2
800 M Breastroke X1	

1,200 M 4 man relay X1 or X2

This makes a total of 21 swimming events.

Table Tennis

Single X1

Doubles X2

Mixed Doubles X1

This makes a total of 3 events table tennis.

Taekwondo X2

There will be 2 events due to different weight classes.

Tennis:

Singles X1

Doubles X2

Mixed Doubles X2

There will be 3 events.

Triathlon X1

Volley Ball X1 or X2

Water Polo X1 or X2

Weight Lifting X2

There will be 10 overall weight lifting events due to different weight classes.

Wrestling "Free Style" X2

There will be 2 freestyle wrestling events due to different weight classes.

Wrestling "Greco" X2

There will be two events due to different weight classes.

As individuals (X1) or together (X2*), Eko and Indra shall be in a total of at least 126 different Olympic Events and may actually compete in more events. The goal of the President of Indonesia is to break the record of total gold medals won by the United States – that was 83 gold medals in the 1984 Summer Olympics. And since then, the President has decided the 2nd most important thing was to win the football (soccer) matches, for the President was to be the manager/coach of the Indonesian Olympic Football Club."

Naturally, none of the sportsbooks and sports betting parlors are taking any action on any event that Eko and Indra will be involved in or may consider participating in. After all, the world's largest casino did lose hundreds of billions of dollars when Eko and Indra took the

Albuquerque Conquistadors. They had been ranked dead last to win the last World Championship Baseball last season during their first/initial season. We all know how that worked out for the sportsbooks.

Now that Eko and Indra will indeed participate in the 2032 Summer Olympic Games in Moscow, the sportsbooks will certainly only accept bets and wagers in women's events, and will not take any bets for any of the men's or mixed (men and women) Olympic events.

Chapter 5
Concerns

It is early February 2032, and the pre-qualifying events are soon to start. Some of the pre-qualifying events are indeed scheduled at the same time, and at times in different locations or even in nearby cities. These pre-qualifying events allow everyone in the games a chance to earn a spot to compete in the upcoming Summer Olympics. Not all of the events at the Olympics may or may not have pre-qualifying *"prior"* to the actual Olympic Games. Yet many do, and this requires a person or team to earn a spot by qualifying in these events before the actual games start.

Eko and Indra believe that they will be able to compete in at least a minimum of 128 events during the upcoming Summer Olympics if they successfully qualify for the events that need any type of qualifying. Yet since Eko and Indra cannot be at two places at the same time, they decided that for the first time ever, they would play separately in order to be qualified as required by the OIC rules. Everyone in the village believed it would be a great thing. That great concern is that Eko and Indra have never been separated. They have always at least been in the presence of each other at the same location.

That separation for a long period of time has never happened. But because of the requirements prior to the actual games, Eko and Indra will have to be in 2 different cities or even countries during these Summer Olympics pre-qualifying and qualifying events. By doing this now and not later, it serves two purposes. First, it gives Indonesia the best chance to make it to the Summer Olympics in the events they believe they can compete at times when Eko is at one place and Indra at another.

That was something that was determined during the time the IOC, Russia, and Indonesia Olympic Representatives all met with scheduling the events to maximize Indonesia's chances. This was the biggest concern of the Indonesian President. The separation of the twin brothers would also lead to more events, more spectators, more media coverage, and more of everything. The best way to ensure this happens is having at least one of the Suparman twins if you can't have both Eko and Indra.

The one important factor is that they can place both Eko and Indra on the official roster for team sports. They can do this even if they both do not participate in the qualifying or pre-qualifying rounds, as long as the team qualifies to participate and win a position for the 2032 Olympics. The other brother would be legal to compete in those games or events since it would be a team-qualifying event and not individual-qualifying events. At this time, both Aspyn and Susan are now close to eight months pregnant. They are both expected to have twins. Since they are only around eight months pregnant, they are at this time not able to travel and be with their husbands Eko and Indra, per doctor's orders, for the due date is coming ever so close at this time.

Aspyn and Susan are aware that this will be the first time either brother has been apart, as is everyone else in the tribe or close to the twins. Even the twins have changed. For the first time since the wedding, they do not have a smile; in just a day, Eko and Indra will indeed be apart from the other for more than 2 weeks, and even longer away from their pregnant wives. It is hard for each brother.

Everyone knew about this, yet no one talked about it. Since it will be the first time ever that Eko and Indra will be traveling separately, they will not even at least have their wives with them. That would have helped if any separation issues were to happen - at this time, no one knows how either Eko or Indra will react to the separation. Idah and Roger will not be joining either one of them during the pre-qualifying events, because the village will need them to take care of all the various humanitarian work worldwide. This is the work that started back in the mid of October.

After all, this does require quite a bit of leadership, and it is very important to everyone involved to continue with the success that is being counted on by the whole world. Eko will have Michael Dean as his security and bodyguard since they will be in different places. Indra will have *"DJ"* Daniel Joe as his security and bodyguard. This decision was decided by the group of Eko, Indra, Idah, Roger, Sheldon, and Barbara after Aspyn and Susan were no longer allowed to travel.

Barbara was now also responsible for also getting additional security for the villagers and everyone else, as well as for having additional personnel to make the trips with Eko and Indra. The divided brothers required more security since they were going to foreign countries during the pre-qualifying events necessary to legally compete in the Summer Olympics.

Most concern isn't for Eko and Indra - after all, they can run so fast you can barely see them. They are, without a doubt, also the strongest people on the entire planet, especially since they have been mastering various forms of self-defense just for some of the Olympic Events. The concern is how the two men will be without the other, or even without their wives during this first series of pre-qualifying events.

The greatest training Eko and Indra have undergone was with Michael Dean and *"DJ"* Daniel Joe. Every day for 45 minutes to up to an hour or so, every single day, they all train together. This way, it also keeps Michael and *"DJ"* in tip-top condition. They are experts in all aspects of self-defense have taught Eko and Indra how to take care of themselves. They have mastered self-defense, yet have never had a need to use this skill at any time. Better to be trained and prepared is what *"DJ,"* thought.

Put all training together, Eko and Indra are the fastest and also strongest humans in the world, second to no one else. They are capable of being lethal, even though both Eko and Indra are certainly non-violent. They are still the same two young men Roger met that first day he encountered them back on the beach that led to this day. The biggest concern is for Aspyn and Susan. After all, only the villagers, the family members of Aspyn and Susan, and a few outsiders even know that Eko and Indra are no longer single but married. Asypn and Susan's pregnancies would indeed create an even greater media demand if they were to travel.

But since they were not making this trip, this was not a concern at this time. They had learned by experience, after all, when playing baseball last year. They would often travel to compete against other baseball teams. Whenever they showed up as the visiting team, the media, fans, and everyone would eventually find out where they were staying. Such a situation in the Olympics could mean an even greater amount of media attention. Even in a city as large as Moscow, where the majority of Olympic events would be held, it wouldn't be long until it was leaked where Aspyn and Susan were staying since both Eko and Indra would be required to stay with the other Olympians at the *"Olympic village."* The Olympic village is where all the athletes, coaches, and trainers from different countries stay.

But the media was after Eko and Indra, as they would be again when they learn of these two pregnant women, the wives of Eko and Indra, and the mother of their children. Now that would create even more hype, attracting non-sports media that would have otherwise stayed away from the Summer Olympics. Once the non-sports media became aware of Susan and Aspyn being married to the world-famous Eko and Indra, not to mention pregnancy, they would be interested in having the scoop about them to share with the customers purchasing their magazines.

This unique opportunity would create an even greater buzz, more than likely exceeding even the time Eko and Indra were first introduced. Yet, Aspyn and Susan will not be on this trip, and probably more trips as more qualifying events occur. Unless they are approved to travel by the doctors, there would be no traveling for either woman. The time for the games to officially begin in Moscow will be during the mid of July. So if Aspyn and Susan were present for them, they would probably not just be the wives of Eko and Indra, but also the mothers of their children. Barbara's biggest concern for Aspyn and Susan is it would be even *"bigger"* news-wise, once it got out that both Aspyn and Susan were carrying twins.

This is why Barbara has been securing more additional full-time security and additional personal bodyguards. Barbara was able to hire people who had personal references from Michael Dean and *"DJ"* Danny Joe. They had trained, been on missions, and had a bond that only those that have served have - that brotherhood that is created by the bonds of working/serving together is something only they understand.

This is especially so since they will be going into different countries outside of Indonesia - the USA or even Australia, where home is now. After all, even though they now live in Australia, it has been *"hidden"* and kept a secret by a few who hope that Australia would remain secret from the rest of the world.

They are now leaving the village to where the transport helicopter is waiting to take them to a private airfield. Everyone that is not going is present, and many are happy, although some are sad in both groups. Idah, Barbara, and even Roger are filled with mixed emotions, joyful but sad to see them all go. Everyone hugs the brothers and gives them advice. Goodbye is something they are not used to saying, so they say *"until next time."*

As they load up everyone in the helicopter, the villagers get as close as they can. Eko, Indra, Michael and *"DJ"* had with them 6 additional trusted bodyguards. Everyone is waving and cheering, knowing that they too will not be with 4 of their villagers: Eko, Indra, Michael, and *"DJ."* Yes, even Michael and *"DJ"* were part of the Family in the village.

EKO & INDRA

Chapter 6
Separation

The group of men from the tribe arrives at the airfield near Sydney, Australia, where Barbara had Sheldon provide two luxury jets. One jet is for Eko, Michael, and three other members of the security detail. They are going to Shanghai, China, for several qualifying events. Indra, Danny Joe *"DJ,"* and the three other members of this security detail are going to Manila and the Philippines for different qualifying events. For the first time ever, as they deport the airfield in Australia for Shanghai, China, and Manila, and the Philippines, Eko, and Indra will be separated by more than a mile or two from the other.

Because of this, and because their wives cannot travel with them, Eko and Indra are not happy. But even though the brothers may be sad, they do the best they can to make sure no one else notices. They know that this will be hard, especially after just getting married and all four of them spending almost all their time together for the last several months. Not only are the brothers sad, but Susan and Aspyn will also be sad and miss their husbands.

This was indeed one of their biggest fears, and it was the right decision to do this prior to the actual games later this Summer, even though they all would be in Moscow. That's because certain events will be held in different cities in Russia and at times require that the twins each go to different cities in order to participate in all the events they want to compete in.

Eko and Michael and the others are scheduled to land first for the trip to Shanghai, China, from Sydney, Australia, for the distance is approximately 2,745 miles away. As for Indra and *"DJ"* Daniel Joe and the others, the flight from Sydney, Australia to Manila, Phillippines is approximately 3,884 miles away and will take nearly two hours longer to arrive because of the distance.

It is announced to everyone in the jet heading to Manila that the others have arrived safely in Shanghai, China, and they are estimating that the arrival time to Manila will be about 2 more hours. As this is being announced, Barbara's cell phone rings. It is Eko to let them all know they have arrived and that he already misses everyone.

Susan asks Aspyn, *"How is Indra doing with the separation?"*

Aspyn replied, "Better than expected, but he is sad and trying to not anyone know, Susan."

"Yes, that is how it is for Eko, too, but together we can make sure they will be fine," responded Susan. "Let us stay strong, so our husbands do not worry about us."

They both agree to be strong, even though they feel alone now that their husbands are gone for two weeks. They wish the other good luck and say their goodbyes. As the jet in Shanghai is at the final stopping point, they see that quite a few security personnel have reached here.

That's because this is the first time Eko and his brother have been in the public eye for the last 5-6 months. It had been leaked that both brothers would at times be making separate appearances during the pre-qualifying, qualifying and even Olympic events; after all, they are attempting to break the all-time Gold Medal record in one Summer Olympics. This is the one and only way to have a chance to achieve this specific goal.

As the door opens in the jet, most in attendance were expecting to see Eko first since everyone knew that Eko being the "oldest, firstborn" would always exit first, and they have always followed that tradition. However, it is Michael who is the first to depart the jet, followed by Eko and the 3 others in the group. Eko was expecting the media to instantly attempt to get closer, as that was always the case. But this time was different. Of course, the media was very much interested in Eko, but this was China, and they remain calm and well behaved.

You could immediately hear the questions:

"Eko, where is Indra?"

"Eko, are you excited for the games?"

"Eko, what are you competing in?"

The questions went on and on, and everyone was now focused on Eko. This was   indeed was a nice change - everyone being completely respectful.

Michael makes a phone call to *"DJ"* on the other plane and tells them how well the arrival was going and hopes that Indra and others will be as fortunate.

And it is more than likely that the media and press over in Milan would have been informed of Eko's arrival in China by now, and that they would know only one brother, Indra, would be landing in Milan. Eko is now standing beside the official greeters and diplomats from the Chinese Olympic Committee.

Most do see Eko, and then the noise from the large group becomes silent as Eko is about to speak to the crowd.

Eko started his speech. "Hello, and thank you all for this lovely reception. My name is Eko Suparman."

After 45 minutes of interviews from various reporters, most of them could tell something was wrong with Eko, and many of them questioned him about how he was feeling. But Eko didn't say anything except, "All is great, happy to be here." He smiled and nodded his head in approval. The noise grew louder, and the group began to grow even larger, moving towards Eko. Eko immediately used his speed to disappear instantly.

In a matter of moments, he had run to the outskirts of town where no one was around. He is sad now and begins to cry, for he is lonely for the first time in his life. Eko then calls Barbara back in Australia to let her know that he is by himself and then asks to speak to Susan. Susan gets on the phone.

"Hello, my love, is everything all right? Barbara told me you are alone."

"Yes, I am alone," said Eko. "I just needed some time to myself. I miss you and   everyone else."

"Stay strong, my love," said Susan. "We are all fine. We miss you too, but this is important. Go and win, Eko."

Hearing Susan's voice made Eko feel much better. He then called Michael to meet him with the security detail. He sat by a small river until he heard a vehicle approaching. It was Michael arriving to pick up Eko. Eko told them all he was fine and just wanted to be there for a little while until things cooled down. Instantly, Michael looked at Eko.

"Eko, we can stay here as long as you want or need."

Now that Indra knows how the landing went for Eko, he and his group are preparing to land in Manila. They decided to take a different approach, which was agreed upon by everyone. Indra would indeed be the first to leave and would be prepared for the masses. Unlike China, where everyone was well behaved, this would be as different as the sun is to the moon. The locals here would be louder, as they consider the Suparman twins to be heroes. To them, they are the superstars the Filipinos admire the most.

Indra departs, and those in attendance were happy. Yes, they are very rowdy and make a lot of noise, but they remain behind the barricades and are delighted to see one of the Suparman Twins. Indra departs the plane, followed by "DJ" and then the others of the security detail.

Indra is hit with the questions based on what is now public knowledge.

"Indra, what do you think about your bother and you being separated?"

"Indra, when are you going to get married? I am single!" This is asked by the female reporters.

After nearly 2 hours of speaking with and engaging the media and press, Indra announces it is time to go, and thanks, everyone. He returns to the jet they had just departed, and they all decide to wait for the media to leave.

In many ways, the occurrence that Barbara was concerned with actually had a very positive silver lining: it forced Eko and Indra to learn to be without the other brother. Plus, their wives would each indeed support their husbands, which would give them the strength they needed to do this by themselves, without the other brother or the support of their wife.

When Aspyn or Susan would speak to their husbands, they would not talk or think about being separated from the other brother for even a second. The separation will make them each stronger. At this present juncture, when they are talking to their wives, both of them are more concerned about their wives and their unborn babies than their brothers.

They are indeed turning into men and will only grow stronger and make their bond even greater. For the very first time, they each realized that their brother wasn't the most important person in their lives, as it had been. Now that they were married, they had to be strong for their family, and they were learning how to do that.

It was now whom they married and their unborn children that were even more important. Yes, Eko and Indra still have that tight bond, that twin relationship that only twins know of. Eko and Indra will always love each other, yet now the love for each of their wives and unborn children is now even greater than the love for one another. This isn't bad; it is life and how things have to be for each family to be successful on their own. And it will be even better for their current goal of getting the most gold medals.

Chapter 7
Shanghai

Eko is at the first qualifying event in Shanghai. With all that has happened, Susan has decided to watch all the events on the huge television screen provided for the entire village, including Aspyn and Susan. They are staying at a highly secret and private location, which has its own security provided by Sheldon for the Suparmans - the wives and everyone in the village. It is a very safe location, and it makes Eko feel comfortable so he can compete without being worried about Susan. Eko didn't need to have any more worries after yesterday.

Archery was won by Eko by winning the overall contest, Eko is qualified for Archery officially. Shooting first with a perfect score each time, he was now the favorite to win this Summer's Olympics in Archery. Basketball had 2 different events for this year's Olympics, with 3 versus 3, as had been played in previous Olympics. The other was the traditional 5 versus 5. It was a 3 team round robin for each event. Round Robin is where each team will play the other team once for a total of 2 games.

If one of the teams wins both of the games, they will automatically be allowed into the Summer Olympics. One of the legal things that Indonesia did was to have Indra listed on the Team. Though Indra is not present for these 4 games, by rostering his name on the team, he would be allowed to compete in the Summer Olympics. Basketball was one of the easiest games for Eko and even Indra, after what they did in Indonesia versus the World's current greatest basketball players. The greatest players couldn't even score a single point. But could this change since it would only be one of the two twins? That was the only question everyone wondered.

After 4 games played, 2 games with 3 on 3 and 2 games with 5 on 5, the results were 4 wins and no losses. However, unlike the way it had been previously, the Team Coach at times did have Eko take a break and sit on the bench, even though he has proven many times in the past that his endurance easily could have stretched out for each and every game. But they decided not to do this. Yet they still did win each game by an average of 72 points. Eko immediately went to the Cycling track for the road marathon. It only took a minute or less for Eko to win this event by using a standard bike. For a man 8 feet 8 inches tall, it was quite a sight to see him on the bike. He looked just like a grown man on a child's tricycle, but he would need to do it not once but twice. Eko finished the Road Cycling within 5 minutes. The next cycling event was *"Track Cycling."* For those that who had not seen Eko at the Road Cycling, they too could hardly believe how Eko managed to fit on the bike. And just like the road event, the track event for Eko completed in less than a minute. Because of the limits of speed and the human eye, technology was created and used in baseball during The Perfect Season.

Ron Levi and Sheldon Winn made sure to expand the nanotechnology for every type of sport to ensure the best performance and correct call each and every time. What some of the other teams thought may be cheating, wasn't cheating at all; it was just that those Suparman twins really are that fast. With that Speed, Eko has it has been very hard for Michael to keep up with him, which made Michael late to all events except for the first one scheduled today - the Archery.

As soon as Eko won the Track Cycling, he is next seen at the Handball Courts. Handball was one of the Russian events added and has two formats: 1 player versus 1 player, and then it is 2 on 2. There are two players per team. Eko is competing in both and is playing the best of 3 games in the

1 on 1, and best of 5 games in the 2 on 2. The first team to get 15 points wins and must win by 2 points. Another way to secure victory is to have a 10 point advantage; for example, 10-0, 11-1, 12-2, 13-3, or 14-4 would all be a 10 point advantage and would be a win. Eko went 2-0 in the matches off 1 versus 1 and scored 20 points, keeping his opponent at a zero score. In the doubles, they won 3-0, but the other team did score a few points when Eko let his Indonesian teammate serve and be more involved.

Eko wanted to make sure that his teammate would be fully involved and only worried about qualifying, which they did again. The last event during this trip was in Rowing. Rowing had several events, and with Eko on the team, Indonesia was able to win each and every rowing competition, and Eko had done what was needed, qualifying Indonesia for all of these events and becoming the favorite to win the Gold too, in all the events he has now qualified for. It has been 36 non-stop hours of these games and events. Eko still remains as fresh as he did during the first event at Archery.

However, he is ready to see Susan and tells Michael he will see him at the residence, before disappearing. Michael sighed. "Not again, he left me, and we are done."

ROGER SCHAFER

Chapter 8
Manila

Indra also started at the same time as Eko did for the Archery since the time zone does not change. Like his older brother Eko, Indra, too, has quite a few pre-qualifying events for the Summer Olympics. Indra is also alone at this time, with only *"DJ,"* Indra's bodyguard. Indra has been strong, yet *"DJ"* knows that he indeed is missing his wife, Aspyn.

The first event for Indra will be badminton. Badminton has two qualifying events for Indra, the first is one versus one. The first team to 15 points winning by two wins the game, and first to win 2 of 3 games wins the event. Indra wins both games by a score of 15-1 for Indra had a serve go too far. The next game was a score of 15-0.

The second badminton was 2 versus 2 with the same rules, except they have to win the best of 5 games. Indra and his Indonesian teammate won 3 straight games by a score of 15-3, 15-3, and 15-2. All of the points that the opponent scored were because of the teammate. Indra was still very much like Eko, even though they were thousands of miles away from the other. Indra wanted his Indonesian teammate to be involved, just like his brother did, even though they were not aware of what each one did. As Indra finished up his last badminton contest, the canoe event was immediately up and minutes from starting. Indra disappeared from the badminton event, only to be next seen at the Canoe events. Canoe had two types of races: Straight and Slalom, and each style had different distances. Plus, Canoe also had single-seated events with one person and double-seated events with two-person events.

Indra, when he first arrived, was disqualified for the first race, for he was not able to get in the right position for the first event/race because of his height at 8 feet 8 inches. But he did manage to eventually get fitted where he was legal and capable of racing. Indra went on to win all the events, as both single and doubles in every category, Straight or Slalom, even though he was disqualified in the very first race.

As soon as the Canoe events were over, Indra had to run to the Fencing Competitions, where he soon to have his first match. This event is the best of 2 of 3 matches and will be in a round-robin with 4 others for a total of 5 in each qualifying group. The top two in each group will qualify for the Summer Olympics. Each of Indra's matches lasted no more than 30 seconds, and this was only allowed for the same nano-technology and the automatic judging based on the scoring. Not only did each match last 30 seconds or less, but not a single person could also even score a point against Indra. Indra, like his brother Eko, had not stopped once during all the previous events. Indra was now at 41 hours of straight competing and was ready to finish this last task so he could go to call and check on his wife, Aspyn. The last event for Indra in Manila was Table Tennis, also commonly referred to as *"Ping Pong."* It is a best of 5 matches, and the winner is the first to 21 or must win by at least 2 points.

Olympic Table Tennis also has a mercy rule where anyone leading or winning by 10 points will be declared the winner. There is a total of 2 qualifying events for Table Tennis; the first is singles match with one versus one, and the other is a doubles match with 2 on 2. Both of these events have the exact same rules. Each event is a five-team round-robin, with the top team guaranteed a spot in the Olympics.

The two teams with the most win, and there's a tie on wins the one with the most points scored, would also be invited to the Olympics. Indra won against all 4 opponents in the singles, winning each game 10-0 and not losing any games or getting scored on. Indra in the doubles won against all 4 opponents, but some of the games did go on longer for his teammate was scored on. Plus, while serving, it was often double scratched to allow points for the team playing against them. However, it was still Indra and his teams that won each and every qualifying event as needed, just as his brother Eko did too. As soon as the match ended, *"DJ."* didn't even ask if Indra wanted a ride, for he knew that Indra would be going straight to call and talk to Aspyn since it has been nearly 2 days since he last saw her. Even though these rounds of the pre-qualifying event have come to an end, each husband immediately left when they were done to go somewhere they could privately call and speak to their pregnant wives to make sure that they were doing fine. To tell them how much they loved and also missed them and everyone else.

Eko and Indra decided that they would each stay a couple of more days to rest and spend time preparing for the next journey of the next round of events. It appears that the issue of being separated is now a thought of the past, and there is no need to worry, for they succeeded and were able to perform and achieve the goals they set out.

The Doctors have agreed that both wives may travel, and it is agreed that they will go to where their husbands are and spend some much needed alone time, for this has been the longest that each of these two couples has been apart. But with the next events happening in Rio De Janeiro, Brazil, instead of heading back to Australia, each group will leave in two days and then all meet together in Rio de Janeiro for the swimming, diving and other water Olympic pre-qualifying events needed to compete in the Summer Olympics.

Chapter 9
Rio de Janeiro

It has been over a week since Eko and Indra were together, and everyone is happy that nothing bad occurred during this time. The twins were so busy with everything, as well as with their pregnant wives that the time passed far quicker than when they had been together or not with their wives. Yet today will be an eventful one and also the first time the other competitors and the rest of the world will see Eko and Indra together.

Barbara made sure that they arrived at an unusual hour when most would be sleeping. They kept knowledge of their arrival times very secretive, so only a few people knew when Eko and Indra would each arrive since they were coming from two different locations Shanghai, China, and Manila, Philippines. Barbara was actually more concerned for Aspyn and Susan, who are now showing even more.

To look at either woman, it is quite obvious they each were pregnant. Yet, only the world isn't aware of Aspyn or even Susan, and no one knows about anything at this time. They also do not know that Indra and Eko are also now married and that both Aspyn and Susan, are each also pregnant and carrying twins. Jorge Paulo Lemann is the richest person in Brazil and a close friend of Sheldon Winn and Barbara Sue, who have had many business relationships and a long friendship with him. Mr. Lemann and his family requested that both Eko and Indra and everyone else would be his guests and under his protection during their stay for this round of pre-qualifying events. Sheldon, of course, informed Jorge about Susan and Aspyn, pregnant wives of Eko and Indra.

The Lemann family, because of the recent media and exposure, were aware of Eko and Indra. The Lemann family was concerned that some South American cartels might be highly interested in attempting to kidnap Aspyn, Susan, or both. Yet when Aspyn arrived with Indra first at the airport, it quickly became obvious that there was more than just Aspyn to be concerned about – the worries had just doubled. Now they will need to make sure both women, Aspyn and Susan, are both safe from any outsiders that may wish them to harm or hold them captive for ransom.

Mr. Lemann immediately called Sheldon, yet Sheldon was not able to directly answer his call. So Mr. Lemann calls Barbara Sue, who does answer. Barbara does confirm the news; after visually seeing Aspyn, it is a secret that can't be silenced. After all, that is why Barbara had both Michael Dean and *"DJ"* Daniel Joe, along with 6 other highly skilled and trained bodyguards and personal security dedicated to Eko, Indra, Aspyn, and Susan. Yet the secret of both Aspyn and Susan was unexpectedly announced and was in the local news and newspapers that next day. On hearing this news, Barbara was upset, for she knew that it was more than likely someone from the Lemann camp, such as an employee or someone close to the Lemann family who must have leaked about Aspyn and Susan.

At this time, they couldn't do anything about it, for it was the truth. So after she had spoken this situation with both Aspyn and Susan, the three ladies decided that Aspyn and Susan were ready to announce that they both were indeed Mrs. Suparman and pregnant with their own twins as well.

Aspyn then asked her husband at the beginning of these qualifying events opening for Indra to announce that he too, is married and that just like Susan, his sister-in-law, his wife Susan, also is pregnant with twins too. This time Susan decided to stay at the residence with Aspyn as well, especially after being warned about all the issues of kidnapping and possible abduction. It would be easier and safer to stay under the constant heavy security protection of the richest and most secured person in all of Brazil.

With the events to start in an hour, Eko, Indra, Michael, *"DJ"* and 20 others from the Lemann security team are leaving the estate of the Lemann family. Some of the men will be going to the 2nd and 3rd events at Fort Copacabana, where all the Water Events (swimming, diving, and water polo) will take place.

It will be a busy 40-48 hours, and Eko and Indra will be very busy with the following events. After all, they had a total of 25 events overall - 21 in swimming, 3 in diving, and 1 for water polo. Yet these events were much happier for Eko, Indra, Aspyn, and Susan; after all, they were all together again.

Swimming:

100 M Backstroke X1, 100 M Breaststroke X1, 100 M Freestyle X1, 1,500 M Freestyle X1, 200 M Backstroke X1, 200 M Breaststroke X1, 200 M Freestyle X1, 400 M Backstroke X1, 400 M Breaststroke X1, 400 M Freestyle X1, 800 M Backstroke X1, 800 M Breastroke X1, 800 M Freestyle, 1,000 M Backstroke X1, 1,000 M Breastroke X1, 1,000 M Freestyle X1, 200 M 4 man relay X2, 400 M 4

man relay X2, 800 M 4 man relay X2, 1,000 M 4 man relay X2, and 1,200 M 4 man relay X2.

Diving:

SpringBoard Diving X1 and Platform Diving X1 2 diving events.

The X2 would be events where both Eko and Indra would be competing, not against the other brother. Most of the world indeed wanted to see Eko and Indra compete against the other to see who the better overall athlete is true. Yet, that was one of the main things they did not want to do - to compete against one another. The water polo would be several matches, and it may be possible that only one of the twins at times will play in these pre-qualifying games. They even considered securing a position in the water polo in the round-robin of 5 different countries. They may even consider this if based on time or skip a water polo match or even two since more teams will be competing in the Summer Olympics.

As both Eko and Indra are preparing for the 1st event, Water Polo, the media, the spectators, and even members of other competing teams are all asking about Susan and Aspyn. Yes, everyone now knows of both Aspyn and Susan, but the one thing that most did not know about

Aspyn and Susan is that they both are pregnant with twins too. Indra goes to the Public Announcer and turns on the microphone. With most of the cameras now turned where Indra is speaking, Indra announces, "Yes, I am married just like my older brother Eko. My wife Aspyn Suparman and I were married recently in a double marriage ceremony with my brother Eko and my sister-in-law Susan. Yes, Aspyn is pregnant, just like Susan is pregnant with my future nephews or nieces, maybe one of each? Yes, Susan is carrying twins, as is the love of my life. My wife, Aspyn, is also carrying twins. My future sons, daughters, or one of each."

The crowd goes wild, the announcers go wild, and now the world is aware that the two greatest athletes of all time will be adding 4 more children to our world very soon. The games are officially underway now, and Eko and Indra lead the Indonesian Water Polo team to shut out by a score of 122-0 in the first match. The score would have been much higher, yet Indra left early to prepare for his swimming meet.

In the past, we were always used to Eko going first, based on tradition, since he was the older of the two. Yet Eko urged his younger brother to break this tradition, and it was time for Indra to go first. Roger, Idah, Sheldon,

Barbara, and everyone else watching is all very proud of Eko for his decision to have Indra go before his older brother for the first time. As planned, they alternated when it came to individual events to ensure that they never competed directly head to head in any of the pre-qualifying events. Yes, the Water Polo did have a few times where only one of the brothers was competing, yet with the other brother not involved, it allowed twice as many events to be accomplished, just as they originally planned.

The last event was the Water Polo finals, and with 3 straight wins, typically by 100 or more points, Indonesia scored in the prior matches with not a single point scored on them during the previous Water Polo events. Eko and Indra, along with the security, decided not to compete in the finals of the last event, Water Polo.

The host team of Brazil won that contest without Eko and Indra participating, yet Indonesia still qualified for water polo and all the other 24 events needed to qualify for the Summer Olympics. The two reasons they decided not to compete in the final water polo were 1) They wanted to leave early to avoid the media, spectators, and even other athletes, and 2) they both had pregnant wives that were getting closer to delivery each and every day. Eko and

Indra missed them and wanted to be with them, so they did just that.

Besides, Eko and Indra shattered every single record in every event they participated in, setting the bar high for every other athlete. After all, Eko and Indra, time and time again, have shown themselves to be the best athletes ever, perhaps including the future too. Eko and Indra knew that they would have 2 free days to spend before they had to fly to the next location for the next events. Mr. Lemann and his family, along with the combined security details, wanted Eko and Indra and everyone else to get a chance to see what Rio de Janeiro is like. Even though it can be dangerous, the country was beautiful. Besides, it was a much-needed break from all the events and traveling, before they had to travel again.

They had a wonderful time with the Lemann family and were pleased to have the chance to meet many different Brazilians from all walks of life. This time together gave them all an opportunity to recover, for the next events were about to start.

Next up would be the qualifying events in Tokyo Japan, and with that long flight ahead, the whole group was looking forward to some rest and relaxation. With Mr.

Lemann and his family being with the Suparman group, they were shown all of Rio in first-class and upscale arrangements. After all, even Mr. Lemann knew that someone in his organization was the one who had leaked the news about Aspyn. Mr. Lemann wanted to make sure they had a wonderful and safe time; he felt it was the least he could do.

Chapter 10
Tokyo, Japan

Eko, Indra, Aspyn, Susan, Michael, *"DJ,"* and the others are now at an airfield with one of Sheldon's jets. They are about to leave Brazil all together to Tokyo, Japan, for more pre-qualifying events for the Summer Olympics. As they all landed from Rio De Janeiro to Tokyo, Japan. They all see many large signs from the windows of the Jet, which was a common sight wherever Eko and Indra were going to. Yet this time, all the signs, or at least the majority of them, were for Aspyn and Susan.

They have all been so busy that they haven't been able to watch any television or even read a paper on the current news events. But 90% of the news coverage was about Aspyn and Susan the other 10% was about Eko and Indra. This has made both Aspyn and Susan the most searched and talked about people in the entire world and broken every record of women searched for on Google and all other search engines that kept track of these types of statistics.

Aspyn and Susan had officially replaced the former number 1 and 2 most searched/talked about people, who previously happened to be *"Eko and Indra."* Eko and Indra now were 3rd and 4th. But keeping it in the Suparman family, they now all ranked 1-4 as the world's most interesting, searched, discussed people in the entire world. They were indeed the very first power couples - the only other power couples were the Royals, King William, and His Wife Queen Katherine, along with Harry and his wife, Megan.

Even the Royals had not ever once been ranked at all four of the top spots 1-4 and never have any other four family members of the same family ever been ranked at 1-4 as the world's most popular, until now. They, the Royals, had before been the closest four to come close, yet even they, with all their popularity, didn't have all top 4 spots together before the Suparmans. Their record had been shattered by at least a billion-plus searches for the first-ever top 4 people.

The Japanese are known for their ultimate respect towards all others, just like the Chinese. Yet the Japanese fans and media couldn't contain themselves, crowd-wise when the Suparman family all arrived. It was similar to when the twin brothers first landed in the United States, and the crowds were even greater than what Eko and Indra had ever seen at any time. So it was decided then that Eko,

Indra, Michael, *"DJ"* and four others of the security detail would be the only ones to leave the jet. After they had departed, the jet and the luggage was transferred. The jet would then be scheduled to depart to an unknown destination. After all, it was of the utmost importance to keep the new location called *"Home"* in Australia a secret to ensure they are safe and unbothered.

Eko and Indra had quite a bit of work ahead of them with all the Gymnastic events - the Judo, Karate, Kayak, and Tennis events that they needed to compete in to qualify for the Summer Olympics fast approaching. This weekend stop in Tokyo, Japan would include events for Gymnastics, Judo, Karate, Kayak, Taekwondo, and Tennis. This was the least amount of events that Eko and Indra have had since they started all the pre-qualifying and qualifying events.

After being on the road for nearly a month, it was best for Aspyn and Susan to go home to Australia for some much-needed rest for both mothers-to-be.

Eko and Indra had a total of 25 events to qualify for this round of pre-qualifying events for the Summer Olympics. Unlike the previous qualifying events, the scheduling here is much more difficult, timing-wise, then they have been used to. This will be another test; after all, during the actual

Olympics, it will be even tighter, schedule-wise. Events may be scheduled at a specific time, and they are often incorrect. Many factors could cause delays, including injury, scoring issues, and official protests, just to name a few.

Gymnastics:

Floor X1, Pommel Horse X1, Still Rings X1, Vault X1, Parallel Bars X1, and Horizontal *"HIGH"* Bar X1

There were 6 gymnastics events in total. Only Eko or Indra would compete in each category - again, many were hoping to see a head to head competition between the twin brothers, but that wasn't about to happen.

Also, they would be competing in the Kayak:

200 M X1, 2 person 200 M X1 or X2*, 1,000 M X1, 2 person 1,000 M X1 or X2*, 4 man 1,000 M this is 10 events total 5 each for *"Spring and Slalom"*

Even though many thought they would have to go head to head, especially with events like Judo, Karate, Taekwondo, and Tennis, they will be competing in separate weight classes and not in the same weight class. As for Tennis, they will only be playing together in Doubles, so that again Eko and Indra will not compete head to head, one brother versus the other brother.

Without Aspyn and Susan to worry about, life was a little easier for Michael and *"DJ"* on the security detail. On the first night, when they arrived, this allowed both Eko and Indra a chance to spend some time together. It has been quite a while since the two brothers have been alone. They both have had their lives change so much, as they became famous, got married, and did things to improve the world where it needed most. Now they were soon to be fathers, but that didn't scare either of them, for they knew all would be fine.

Twenty-five events are what Eko and Indra need to qualify for here in Tokyo, Japan. One lesson learned was to go to the kayaks, both the single-seaters and double-seaters, to see if they can legally fit in and not be disqualified as had happened in one race in the Canoe events. It was a good thing, Eko, and Indra did this before the actual event, for they discovered that two identical twins, both 8 feet 8 inches tall, could not fit into the double-seater together; it is impossible. So all 2-person events in the kayak events will mean just one of the Suparman Brothers will compete with another teammate from Indonesia.

The brothers decided that Eko would represent for the gymnastic events and the Tennis events, which would 9 total events - six for gymnastics (Floor, Pommel Horse, Still Rings, Vault, Parallel Bars and Horizontal *"HIGH"* Bar.) This leaves three for Tennis singles, doubles, and mixed doubles. These 9 events will keep Eko very busy, especially since they are close to one another. But there is enough time to squeeze in the other events: single man-to-man competition of Judo, Karate, and Taekwondo. Besides, Indra has proven he is very capable in a small kayak, as he has more experience from the canoe qualifying earlier this year. Indra, with his previous experience on the canoes, would be doing all of the kayaking with 10 events overall in the Slalom and Straight, and five races in both Slalom and Straight.

Yet single-seated and double-seated would be another factor as would the distance of these events. Having these 10 events to achieve will leave Indra to have to qualify for Judo, Karate, and Taekwondo, at a different weight class than his brother as well. That way, Eko, and Indra, as designed, would not directly compete against the other.

The one thing officially changed and announced by the OIC *"Olympic International Committee "* was that Eko and Indra, in the individual events based on weight classes, could not then compete in more than one weight class. This would make it fairer for other Olympians. Eko and Indra would be competing at the NO LIMIT: Weight Class and the Super Heavy Weight class, which is 360 pounds or less, even though they barely weighed 272 pounds each. It seems like a lot of weight, but at 8 feet 8 inches tall, they were as thin as they were strong and fast. Even with this official change, it would mean they still have 6 more events overall between the two of them, which is 3 each. Eko would be the No Limit weight class contestant in the Judo and Taekwondo events, and Indra would be the No Limit weight class contestant for the Karate event. That way, Indra would compete in the Super Heavy Weight Class for the Judo and Taekwondo events. Eko would be the Super Heavy Weight Class for the Karate event.

Had this change not been made, Eko and Indra could have competed in the Heavy Weight class and the Super Light Heavy Weight Classes in all three of these sports. Meanwhile, back home in Australia, Aspyn and Susan are with Barbara, Idah, and Roger since he has returned for a brief break. Aspyn and Susan now are very well aware of the recent World Changes and how they are on every news, radio, and internet blog regardless of the language spoken in our vast world.

The doctors are checking on both pregnant women and their unborn twins. Everyone catches up on recent events. Roger tells them how well the foundation is going and wishes he could be more involved with the Olympics. Idah tells everyone how much they were all missed and how she is glad that at least they are all together.

Barbara is thankful everyone is doing well, especially the babies, since the doctors just informed both Aspyn and Susan that the due date is looking to be March 16th. Roger has been listening, yet also watching the current events. He sees how well Eko is doing in the Gymnastic events, scoring perfect scores. No one, man or woman, has been able to do twists, jumps flips, turns, and heights like him, and he is never doing before attempted routines.

As he knows everyone is watching, Roger changes the channel to see Indra, who, as the last kayak race comes to an end, is dominating every aspect of the Kayak. When they are interviewed, Eko always says, "I miss everybody, especially you, Susan." Indra also does the exact same thing, saying, "I miss everybody, especially you, Aspyn."

Everyone is cheering, for since all the villagers have television and computers, they too have followed the entire path of the family members "Eko and Indra." But like everyone else, the villagers are more concerned about Aspyn and Susan. When it is announced that both women are due to have the birth of their children around March 16th, the cheers are even louder. The tennis matches were best of 5 in all three of the different Tennis events: the Singles, Doubles, and Mixed Doubles.

Eko and his teammates for the Doubles and Mixed Doubles matched what Eko did in the Singles. They won 3 straight games, with not a loss of any game, and more importantly, not a single point was scored against them, even in the doubles and mixed doubles with men and women.

Eko and Indra were down to the last 3 events: Judo, Karate, and Taekwondo. Eko and Indra being pleasant, non-violent people, easily could have won each and every match by Knock Out, yet because they do have scoring for all three of these events, they used their speed and not their strength. But they did dominate as expected and won each and every event. Eko and Indra wanted to show respect for those they competed against, even though their competition was heavy disadvantaged and really had no chance to win. They wanted to be respectful and did.

The final event was happening for Eko and Indra in Tokyo, Japan. *"DJ"* brings his cell phone and gives it to Indra, since Eko is finishing his last Taekwondo match in the NO LIMIT Division. Indra says, "Hello, this is Indra." On the other end, it is Aspyn. "Hello my love, congratulations to you and Eko! We have been watching all your events."

Indra said, "How are you doing, my love? How is everyone? Your babies and Susan's babies?"

There was a pause, and then Indra hears crying from Aspyn. He grew concerned. "What is wrong? What is wrong, my love?"

Aspyn said, "Indra, I am not sad, nor am I crying, even though I miss you very much. Love of my life, I am crying, for I am happy. Indra, you see, our babies are all doing wonderfully."

Indra smiled. "That is wonderful news. We shall be leaving Tokyo soon in an hour or so."

Aspyn said, "Indra, our babies and Eko and Susan's babies are all due to be born on March 16th, the same day!"

Indra screams so loud that Eko instantly goes to where Indra is at. Indra then says, "Goodbye, my love. Please give the phone to Susan as I give this phone to Eko."

Eko asked, "What is wrong, brother? What made you scream as you did? I never heard you do that before."

Indra, smiling, hands the phone to Eko, who put the phone close to his ear and could hear Susan's voice. "Hello, my dear wife," he said. "How are you, and what did Aspyn say to make Indra scream as he just did?"

Susan said, "We all heard Indra's scream over here, both on the phone and the TV a few moments later due to the live feed delay! Eko, my Husband, do not fear for what you heard. I shall just tell you. We are all fine. Everyone is fine: the babies, Aspyn, and her babies and everyone in the village."

Eko said, "Then why did Indra make that noise?"

Susan laughed and said, "Because he just found out that his twins will be born on March 16th, and our twins will also be born on March 16th as well."

Eko too makes the same screaming noise as his brother just made a few moments ago.

Susan laughs as they heard Eko's scream of joy on the phone and then a few moments later on the delayed feed from the television. Anyone present at the events in Tokyo must have thought that Eko and Indra were receiving bad news.

Yet, when "DJ" is handed back his phone, some people overheard Eko and Indra excitedly discussing the news of both women having twins each on the exact same day March 16th. It is announced over the Public Address to everyone in attendance and watching. Now the whole world now knows that Eko and Indra, the World's Greatest Twin Brother and Athletes, were each to have their own twins on the same day, i.e., March 16th.

The crowd erupts in cheers, and then a chant begins, "Aspyn, Susan, Aspyn, Susan," over and over again in joy.

Chapter 11
Time Off

The Tokyo, Japan events are now all completed. With the news Eko and Indra received about their wives' due date, the twin brothers decided to go back home to Australia where the village is located. Their arrival in Sydney, Australia, is at a very private Air Field to ensure no one is aware of the new place called Home. Both Eko and Indra were so excited that instead of being transferred on a helicopter, they ran all the way home to the village from where they landed.

Everyone was excited that Eko and Indra were back, and they were so excited that they each rushed to their home to check on their Wives. Yet no one was present, so they immediately went to the medical center set up for all the villagers. Aspyn, Susan, Idah, and Barbara were all there. Everyone is happy to be reunited and together again.

Eko and Indra then sit down, and each is grinning from ear to ear, very happy to be home and catching up with everyone, learning what was happening with the pregnancies as well as any news while they were gone. However, most of the villagers were more excited to hear about all the recent trips. Everyone had missed Eko and Indra, and they were glad to have them home so they could all spend time together. After a long reunion, it was getting late. With Aspyn and Susan both very pregnant, they each are showing signs of being tired. Barbara suggests to everyone that it is time to call it a night and for the two couples to go home and get some rest. Idah agreed, and being the Leader of the village, everyone did exactly that.

Eko and Indra's separate homes are side by side to one another; after all, they still are very close, as close as two brothers or two sisters can be. Now that they are married, they each were very happy to spend time alone together. Aspyn and Susan certainly wanted to know more about the time in Tokyo, Japan, and to be able to be with their husbands.

Yet Eko and Indra were more excited to hear everything about the babies and what the doctors told them. Both couples agreed they did not desire to know the sexes of the babies in advance. Both women are pregnant, both with twins, and both have been informed that they will probably share the same day to deliver on March 16th. The odds of this happening, IF it does, would indeed be a billion to one or greater, for both women to have not only twins but to share the date of birth for all four children.

They eventually fell asleep, which was needed, especially for Eko and Indra, after all the non-stop events and travel. When the two brothers woke up early with little sleep, they were excited to see that Roger was still present and had yet to leave to ensure all the work for the foundation to help others was going as expected and designed. Roger is sitting near the campfire with a cup of coffee, reading some documents. As Eko and Indra approach, Roger sees them and says, "Hello Eko and Indra. It is great to see the two of you. Congratulations on the wonderful news that everyone in the world now knows."

Eko and Indra, both smiling very happily, reply, "Nice to see you, Roger."

Indra then asks, "Roger, you said everyone in the world - what did you mean?"

Roger then shows both of the young men the articles he was reading. Every article was about how the world is now aware of Eko and Indra being married to Aspyn and Susan. They're also aware of the confirmation "slip" about each of these ladies being pregnant with twins and the amazing possibility that both women may have their deliveries on the same day, March 16th.

Roger's cell phone is ringing and notices that the call is from Sheldon Winn. Roger answers the phone. "Hello Sheldon, how are you?"

Sheldon replied, "Good morning, Roger. Well, at least it is morning in Australia. I didn't call you too early, did I?"

"No, Sheldon, as a matter of fact, Eko, Indra, and I were just catching up."

Sheldon said, "Great timing, then. Roger, I called to see if you were aware of the most recent events and news?"

"Yes Sir Sheldon, as a matter of fact, that is what we have been talking about. Hold on, Sheldon, I am going to put you on speakerphone."

Eko and Indra can hear Sheldon now and say, "Hello." Sheldon now has the complete attention of the three men. "Gentleman, as you can see, we have a HUGE event that is now public knowledge," said Sheldon. "I know you all are very well aware of how the press and media do things, so I want to extend my help anyway I can. If you need to get away, I will be more than happy to make sure everyone is safe and that my future godchildren have the best doctors."

Eko and Indra are confused and whisper to Roger, "What are godchildren?"

Roger looks at them and whispers back, "I will tell you when Sheldon is finished."

Each Twin nods their head. Sheldon has finished his conversation, and everyone thanks him for the offer of help and assistance. Roger then explains what he meant. "Godparents are a man and woman, sometimes a couple, who assume responsibilities for the children if something happens to the parents."

Eko said, "That is quite an honor, but what if Susan and I wanted you, Roger and Idah, to be the Godfather? Would we be able to do that?"

Roger nodded. "Yes, Eko, you and Susan will choose and decide whom you wish to have as Godparents."

Eko said, "OK, Roger, it will be you and Idah for my children."

Indra then said, "Roger, would it be ok if Aspyn and I have Sheldon and Barbara as our children's Godparents?"

"Of course," said Roger. "And I am very sure we all would be more than happy and honored to your Godparents. But I do suggest both of you check with your wives first, too."

It is agreed that Eko will speak with Susan as Indra will speak with Aspyn, and see who they want for Godparents.

By this time, everyone in the village is up, and everyone is joyful to have Eko and Indra home. It will be a short trip, with more Summer Olympic events still needing to be completed in the pre-qualifying events. As breakfast is served, it is nice to see how life here is so different than anywhere. Home here is truly similar to the village they had lived on for many decades, for all of Eko and Indra's lives until last year.

After breakfast, Eko, Susan, Indra, Aspyn, Idah, and Barbara will speak and check in with the Doctors at the medical center for all the villagers. They run a few tests and make sure everything is fine for both mothers and all four children. Everything is well. The doctor then informs everyone, "Yes, it does look like March 16th will be the day. We have everything here for anything needed for the births. I know none of you wish to know the gender, or should I say genders of the children so we will not reveal them and promise to keep it that way."

The news is great, and they go out to spend the day together. Eko and Susan go on their own, as do Indra and Aspyn to spend much needed private time. After all, the twins will have to be leaving soon to the next place to qualify. The few days off went by quicker than most days. After making use of their chance to rest and spend time together, Eko and Indra are ready to go to the next City – London, England - for the next series of qualifying events.

Chapter 12
London, England

The King and Queen of England, William, and Katherine had arranged for Eko, his wife Susan, and Indra and his wife Aspyn to be guests when they arrived in London for the much-anticipated Football qualifying. This is the one and only event that Eko and Indra have to win in their Group *"B."* It was wonderful news to everyone in England that the English Football Team was in Group *"A"* and would not have to face Eko and Indra's Indonesian Football Team.

The team was managed by the Indonesian President, who, like King William and Prince Harry, were huge football fans. After all, with Eko and Indra, it made anyone managing/coaching look like a genius. The events would comprise a total of 5 days, with every team having to play 1 game per day. The top 2 winners would be guaranteed a position for the Summer Olympics. With three groups <A>, <B> and <C>, each with 6 teams, there was a total of 18 countries competing. A total of 8 teams overall - the top 2 in each Group and then 2 other teams - would qualify.

England is considered the birthplace of modern football as we know it. Because of the popularity of the sport there, and with many locations to choose from to have the football matches, England was perfect for this event and would ensure all stadiums would sell out because of the strength of the fan base.

Many of the fans will support their National Team. With Eko and Indra in some of the matches when Indonesia plays, it will give many fans a chance to see them live. After all, even with television broadcasts, they can slow the speed of the film so the audiences can view the action. When slowed down, one can see what Eko and Indra are capable of, since most can't see them at full speed. In real life, without slowed down footage, it is like night and day.

With eighteen teams and eight spots open, the fans were getting very excited. Even though Eko and Indra did compete in a charity game against the world's best last fall, quite a few of the English fans still believed that England could compete with Indonesia. With both Clubs being in different groups, that match could only happen in these Summer Olympics, depending on what the groups consist of. After all, this was only for European and Asian teams here in England, and many other countries would be participating in other parts of the world at the same time.

When the entire team arrived, Eko, Susan, Indra, and Aspyn were not on the same jet as the rest of the team. After all, the team flew from Jakarta, Indonesia. Very few people knew where Eko and Indra actually lived, and so they had to leave Sydney, Australia, to meet the rest of the football players in England since even the Indonesian teammates didn't know where Eko and Indra lived or called home. The one and the only person who knew was the President who was to be the Manager during the football matches, and he knew very well to keep silent.

King William and Queen Katherine, along with their children, knew too well about unruly fans and the media, which at times could be even worse than the rabid fans. The King and Queen invited Harry, Megan, and Archie as well to go and meet the Suparman twins and their wives. This was because everyone else was busy at the International Airport, waiting for Eko and Indra to arrive since they were not on the plane with the other teammates. This was something that both Aspyn and Susan did wish to do; they wanted a chance to meet the Royals. So even though they are both closer to the birth of their children, they were cleared for this trip by Dr. Vegarra and the other Doctors. Also on the plane with Eko and Indra were Idah, Barbara, Michael Dean, and *"DJ"* Daniel Joe.

With the security the Royals had along with the Doctors readily available for anything, including delivering babies, this was a chance in a lifetime, even though for Eko and Indra, it was just new people to meet. Idah even knew how important this opportunity was. Barbara, of course, had previously met all four: King William, Queen Katherine, Harry, and Megan, and knew them for many years because of Sheldon Winn.

As they depart from the plane, Barbara exits the plane first. , with their children, all of whom Barbara knows. The children are so excited to see Eko and Indra - after all, they were very well aware of the twin brothers, as were King William and Harry, his younger brother.

Queen Katherine and Megan were excited to meet Aspyn and Susan, and Aspyn and Susan were very excited to meet the Queen and Megan, who they had known of for most of their lives, yet never met. When Eko and Indra left the plane, they saw all the children, and even though they were now 20 years of age, they still were very much like happy children themselves. Everyone meets one another. For the first event, they go to Buckingham Palace to have a meal and see the historical buildings. The Palace is closed during this time because of Eko and Indra and the others in their group. That way, they can go to every room and see things most people will never see, and spend time as they would if they were still at home. After all, the King and Queen, along with Harry and Megan, have been followed by the media and fans since they were born. Actually, the four Royals were very happy not to be the top three of four most-followed people alive any longer. That is now held by Aspyn, Susan, Eko, and Indra, followed by Harry, Queen Catherine, Megan, and Lady Gaga. After Lady Gaga is King William.

If the media were to know that the most-followed 8 of 9 people in the entire world were together, it could end in chaos and cause a lot of havoc, which no one wants. After an eventful dinner of pure enjoyment and a very high-class royal treatment, the women decide that they will spend the evening together. That allows King William, Harry, Eko, Indra, and the children to spend an evening together, getting to know one another.

It is wonderful, for this is the first time in a long time that Aspyn, Susan, Idah, and even Barbara have had anyone other than the villagers or members of the security detail around them. Having two other high-profile women who had encountered the nosy media during their pregnancies was a great experience since they would be more than happy to help Aspyn and Susan with some pointers and information based on their own personal experiences.

One thing that the children, along with King William and Harry learned, was that English food did indeed give both brothers gas. The children ran laughing past the women, and Megan asked, "Why are you all running? What is so funny?"

Harrison said, "Mom, we just heard Eko and Indra fart! They are the loudest, longest and also the stinkiest farts ever."

Everyone giggles and Queen Katherine says, "Well, at least we know they are human."

Harry and his brother are walking quickly, both coughing and laughing at the same time.

After a wonderful evening and a great night of sleep, it is now time for the first matches to start today. With 9 matches per day in the round robins for all the teams, England was very busy, even more so than for the football playoffs. Millions of people are here to view and support their teams, and/or also to see Eko and Indra.

It was a sight to see how many people of all ages from different parts of the World were wearing the Indonesian

Jerseys with either Eko's number *"0"* or Indra's number *"00."* At least half the stadium was wearing one of those Jersey's *"0"* or *"00"* at all the matches. It was the same in the streets and everywhere else.

Each and every match that Indonesia played in was attended by King William, Harry, and their children. However, all the women – Queen Katherine, Megan, Aspyn, Susan, Idah, and Barbara – were doing other things. If one didn't know any better, they would think that these six women have been friends forever. This was very important: the time, the talks, the advice that was shared. And each day, the friendships only grew greater and stronger. It is now the last day of these qualifying matches, and Indonesia has been perfect. So far, they have won all four matches, and not a single goal has been scored on them.

Actually, the opposing teams have yet to get the ball even into the offensive side of the field. The last match of the events didn't even have Eko or Indra compete, and the Indonesian team did lose 5-0.

The final goal differential for Indonesia was 472 goals for and 5 goals against, which only happened in the final match. Even with a match lost, Indonesia had won their bracket in the group they competed in. England also won their group play as well. This made everyone happy, and with such strong friendships made, they would be looking forward to spending time together in Moscow during the Summer Olympics.

Harry joked, "Eko and Indra, you're our friends, so if you play England take it easy on them, OK?"

Everyone laughed, especially the children. Then the young prince said, "You do know that Eko and Indra could win any sport simply by gassing the other team." Everyone laughed again.

It was getting close to the time to depart. Two jets would be departing, one for Eko, Indra, Michael, and DJ to go to the next qualifying events, and the other jet for Aspyn, Susan, Idah, and Barbara to go back home as per the doctor's orders at Buckingham Palace. Yes, it is now even closer to March 16th, and this far in the pregnancy, the women would soon need to be home full-time with no more travel after this until after the babies are born.

Chapter 13
Mumbai, India

The brothers fly directly from London, England to Mumbai, India, for their next three events: boxing, cricket, and weightlifting. It would be a quick visit to qualify for these three events, especially since they could only compete in one weight class for the boxing and weightlifting events that needed qualifications for the Olympics.

As the four men: Eko, Indra, Michael, and *"DJ"* leave the jet that landed at the private state airfield, they were met by the President and the Prime Minister of India with a very small detail of the security. Because it is a parliamentary democratic republic, India has a President who is the Head of State and a Prime Minister who is responsible for running the federal government.

These are the two most powerful people in India. Each man has specific areas that they each are in charge of. Eko and Indra met both the President and the Prime Minister, who welcomed the Suparman twins. Both men were sad that Aspyn and Susan could not make the journey, but they were aware that the women were so far along in the pregnancies that their travel had been limited. Arriving early before any of the scheduled events, the President and Prime Minister request Eko, Indra, Michael, and *"DJ"* to accompany them on a tour of India via helicopter. India is the second most populated country in the entire world; only China has a larger population than India. With so much to see and given how the huge population will cause the roads and streets to be heavily crowded, it is determined that the best method of travel for Eko and Indra will be via helicopter to and from the events.

The first stop was the most famous of all attractions in India, the Taj Mahal. The Taj Mahal is an ivory-white marble mausoleum on the southern bank of the Yamuna River in the Indian city of Agra. It was commissioned in 1632 by the Mughal emperor, Shah Jahan, to house the tomb of his favorite wife and is the most famous of all attractions in India. Eko and Indra are very impressed; they have seen many iconic buildings, but this touched them, and they informed the President and Prime Minister that the Emperor must have loved his wife as Eko loved Susan and Indra loved Aspyn.

The tour is not private, yet the tourists visiting as well as the locals from India are very respectful and do not make a scene or go wild at the sight of Eko and Indra. After that, they decide to go and see more of India's famous places: Amber Palace, Hawa Mahal, Agra Fort, Humayun's Tomb, Jama Masjid, and Jim Corbett National Park. Each place was beautiful and very interesting. The Prime Minister asked Eko and Indra, which they liked the most and why. They replied the National Park for Tigers and Wildlife was wonderful and their favorite. Eko then asked the President and Prime Minister, "When the Olympics are done, can Indra and our families come back to visit, especially the park with the tigers?" Both, The President and Prime Minister replied, "Both of you and your families are indeed most welcome, and we look forward to the day we can meet them all.

We also extend an open invitation to the two men that have guns and weapons with us, Michael and "DJ." After a day of sightseeing and with the events now less than a day away, the group returns to Mumbai for the evening as the 1st cricket match is the next morning. Cricket to India is what football is to England and what baseball is to America.

It is their most followed sport, second to none. Here are the rules of Cricket. Cricket is played by two teams of 11, with one side taking a turn to bat a ball and score runs, while the other team will bowl and field the ball to restrict the opposition from scoring. The main objective of cricket is to score as many runs as possible against the opponent. Typically, test and first-class cricket matches are played over three to five days, with at least six hours of cricket being played each day. List A matches last for six hours or more, and 20 and 100-ball matches last just a few hours. For the Olympic qualifying and the actual Olympic Cricket Matches, there will be 100 ball matches.

The format will be a round-robin as it is in many of the pre-qualifying and qualifying events. The Indonesian team will have 3 Matches; it did not draw India, which made the Indian President and Prime Minister quite happy. After all, they did win in the first match, and not a single point was earned when Indonesia won the 1st of 3 Matches. With the match over, the twin brothers, along with Michael and "DJ," are going to the Boxing event.

Both brothers will be competing in the Unlimited Class as well as the Super Heavy Weight Class, as agreed upon, even though they could compete in several other lower weight classes since the ruling by "OIC" Olympic International Committee was that an athlete could compete in higher weight classes if they choose or their actual weight class. But they cannot compete in two different weight classes. Back in the 2000 Olympics, Olympic bouts changed from three rounds of three minutes to four rounds of two minutes for the Games at Sydney in 2000 and have been that way since 2000.

All boxers are required to use headgear, yet even with extra protection and the 4 rounds at 2 minutes per round, most are expecting all of Eko and Indra's matches to be 1st Round Technical Knock Outs, commonly referred to as "TKO's." And yes, the experts were indeed correct, for the boxing events were all done and finished in the 1st round and only required one "tap" for Eko and Indra to win the boxing match.

Even though it would be the fight of a lifetime, Eko and Indra would not be matched up against the other. Yet that didn't stop the fans and media from constantly bringing that up. And since they each were in separate weight classes, there was no way this dream fight was to happen during this year's Olympic Games.

The following day was the second of 3 games in cricket, and the results were the same – the game lasted 52 minutes, but the opposing team remained scoreless. Two days in a row and not a single point was awarded to the teams that had cricket matches against Indonesia. Upon completing this, it was time for the second boxing matches, and this time Eko and Indra decided to try a different approach suggested by Michael and "DJ." This time, they were going to allow the Eko and Indra's opponents a fair chance – the brothers would not avoid taking punches and would not even punch back in the 1st round. Naturally, the only ones aware of this were the four men, Eko, Indra, Michael, and "DJ." It did indeed give the fans present a chance to see how strong the twins were. The punches landing on the twins felt to them as if they were being attacked by houseflies. By the second round, each only needed tap each to win by "TKO" Technical Knock Out.

The third event today, weightlifting, would be one day only — the Big Two. The "classic lifts" are the two staples of the Olympic weightlifting competition: the clean and jerk, and the snatch. The derivatives for weightlifting are a front squat, overhead squat, power clean, muscle snatch (from mid-hang), push press, and the high pull (from mid-hang) lifting events, which are the weightlifting events. There are nine different events for both Eko and Indra, and they also have a Gold Medal in the Olympics for the overall top combined scores of the 9 events, which could mean a total of 20 gold medals just in weightlifting.

Eko and Indra were able to tie the other brother in all 9 events. What was amazing was that the bar only had so much room and a maximum weight it could take because of the length of the number of weights that can be added. On each and every technique, both brothers had the maximum amount of weight possible based on the size of the bar. To show off, they even only used one hand in several of the competitions/lifts. How strong are Eko and Indra? It was something that still couldn't be measured. The technology to find out will need to be improved in the near future. By the time the Olympics are in full swing, Ron Levi will have a fix so the world can find out what Eko and Indra are capable of when it comes to weightlifting. After witnessing the feats of strength, it is certain the two strongest men, without any question, are Eko and Indra. Roger was able to see this event, even though he was not present.

It reminded him of the time he first met Eko and Indra on the beach. He remembered how he first discovered them when they picked a huge boulder that must have weighed several thousands of pounds, moved it effortlessly, and secured his parachute. Seeing this, Roger immediately called Ronald Levi and informed Ron that they would need to have a better way for the Olympics. Ron certainly agreed and knew this would be something he could improve. After all, Ron was also watching these events, as was everyone else.

Finally, the last day of the events was here. There was one more cricket game to play, which again lasted only 46 minutes. Not a single point was scored against Indonesia - they were 3-0. Indonesia had succeeded in its efforts to make it to the Summer Games.

The boxing matches were both done in less than 2 seconds. When the bell rang to signify the beginning of the match, the eight feet eight-inch tall twins just tapped their opponents and again won by the "TKO."

When Eko and Indra both finished, "DJ" asked them, "Why so quick this time?"

Eko replied, "Because we are ready to finish this so we can go back to our wives."

Michael smiled and said, "I certainly understand."

"Well, we are done," said Indra. "Let us thank our hosts, the President, and Prime Minister, and get back home."

Both Eko and Indra thanked the President and Prime Minister, and they did apologize for showing off during the weightlifting events when they used just one arm, for Idah didn't approve of how they had competed. With heads bowed downwards, they asked the leaders to accept their apologies.

Eko said, "My brother and I are sorry for how we acted and do apologize."

The Prime Minister laughed. "Do not worry," he said. "For you are both young. We appreciate your apology and will tell all the others in the weightlifting how you feel."

Indra asked, "Can we come back, too? We heard you have many places with tigers and other animals and would like to see them too."

"You all are welcome to India anytime you wish, and please bring your family too," said the President of India.

They all shook hands and said their goodbyes.

EKO & INDRA

Chapter 14
Excitement

After the trip from India, they are finally back home. Even though it was one of the shortest trips since this Olympic journey started, all that Eko and Indra could think of at every moment is for their pregnant wives and unborn children. As March 16th nears, they become more restless and even start to lose focus on normal daily tasks.

For Eko and Indra, family has always been the most important thing, especially now that they have their own family in addition to their extended family in the form of all the villagers. After all, they still are human. Even though they may appear to superhuman, they still are just two young men that are 20 years of age.

As they are reviewing the last of the events that will need to be completed, they notice that one qualifying event may have to be without Eko and Indra. The brothers would not compete in events scheduled around March 16th, the day when their children are to be born if the doctors are correct. March 16th would be the 3rd day of 5 days for the baseball qualifications. Baseball was the sport that made them famous, but it was going to be an event they would not be involved in, for it did indeed conflict with when the babies are to be born. No matter what, they would be present in the village that day and near those days. They could not miss this special day for anything, even for baseball or any other sport or contest.

Barbara agreed as did Idah, and of course, Aspyn and Susan. After all, everyone was expecting the fathers to be present when the birth of children happen. March 16th was the target/expected date of birth, but it still could be a day or two, earlier or later. Idah even stated that since she had been the leader, the father would be present during the births of their babies. Every tribe member, including Barbara, fully agreed.

Barbara thought that Sheldon would not be happy. Baseball had been great for Eko, Indra, and the entire tribe. Even if they were to represent Indonesia, Eko and Indra would always also be known as Conquistadors Baseball Players, especially what they did in what is now called "The Perfect Season."

Sheldon's reaction to the news was the opposite of what Barbara thought. Sheldon actually didn't want Eko and Indra to play baseball for any other team except his baseball team, the Albuquerque Conquistadors. Sheldon told Barbara this during this conversation but requested that Barbara keep that between herself and Sheldon. The news of how well Aspyn and Susan were doing was more important, and Sheldon told Barbara that Roger, Ron, Bill, and the best baby doctors would be at the village no later than March 10th. They would also stay a few days beyond the birth of the Suparman children.

As the phone conversation was coming to an end, Barbara said to Sheldon, "Sheldon, I am going to have Idah tell the President of Indonesia our decision. As Leader, her relationship with the President will make it better for Eko, Indra, and everyone else."

It is agreed. They say their goodbyes and end the phone call.

Idah heard her name as the conversation just ended. She asked Barbara, "Barbara, was that Sheldon? I heard my name being mentioned. What did you two want of me?"

Barbara then told Idah what she and Sheldon thought of the births of the Suparman children conflicting with the Baseball qualifying events. She said they both thought the event should not include Eko and Indra because of the conflicting dates and the location. Without a second thought, Idah completely agreed. She knew just how Eko and Susan, and Indra and Aspyn would become sad when the other was gone. When giving birth, parents should be happy and excited, not sad, and lonely. For Idah, a baby's birth should be a completely positive experience with positive energy so the children will grow up happy.

Eko, Indra, Aspyn, Susan, Barbara, and Idah discussed the oversight and talked about how the clash between the baseball qualifying even and the date of the birth had not noticed until today. The entire group fully agrees, and not a single one of them wants it any other way except as discussed.

Now that it is 100% agreed, it is time for Idah to make the phone call to the President of Indonesia and let him know the news as well. Eko, Indra, Aspyn, Susan, and Barbara were all present as Idah called the President to inform him of the news.

Idah dialed the number, and the phone is answered in the first ring by the President. The President said, "Hello Idah, it is me, the President. How are you and everyone doing?"

Idah replied, "Everyone is well. Everyone is excited that we are close to adding more family in our village." The President said, "Well, that is excellent news. So the women and babies are all healthy. What of our twins? How are they doing?"

Idah paused. "Well, Mr. President, I am calling you on behalf of Eko and Indra."

Immediately the President grew concerned. "Is something wrong with Eko or Indra? What is it that they need?"

Idah looked at the others, hearing the conversation. Indra then motioned to Idah to give him the phone. Idah handed the phone to Indra, who said, "Good day, Mr. President. It is I, Indra, and with me is Eko. Both of us are calling to let you know that we will not be involved in the Olympics..."

The President immediately interrupted, "WHAT DO YOU MEAN? You will not be involved in the Olympics? YOU BOTH PROMISED!" He sounded both very concerned and very upset. Eko then said to the President, "No, Mr. President, we will keep our promise. But we will not be qualifying for the baseball part because our babies are to be born then, and we both will be with our wives during birth."

The President released a sigh of relief. "Phew! Well, we can always have your wives at the location and make sure they are well taken care of. That way, we can do both - you boys can make it to the games, and you can even miss part of a game to be with your wives during the birth, of course."

Idah now has the phone. "No, that will not happen, Mr. President. It is not what we, we as in all of us, want. Eko and Indra will be here, and the wives will not be traveling since they're pregnant. The babies are to be born here in our village."

Hearing this, the President agrees. After all, the President knows that with or without the Olympic Baseball games, he needs both Eko and Indra. So it is agreed and the one sport everyone expected to see Eko and Indra play, baseball, was the one Olympic Event that they would not be playing.

Without Eko and Indra, Indonesia will have little chance to qualify, especially based on the teams that will be in the pre-qualifying round-robin games.

Chapter 15
Seoul, Korea

The Asian Athletics Championships for Track and Field Summer Olympics will be held at the Incheon Munhak Stadium. Korea has been one country for the last eight years. No longer is there a North or South Korea, but just one nation that will be home to the 2032 Asia Track and Field Qualifications for the Summer Olympics.

Eko and Indra have many events to qualify for here:

Athletics (also known as) Track and Field

Track: 100 M X1, 200 M X1, 400 M X1, 800 M X1, 1,500 M X1, 5,000 M X1, 10,000 M Marathon X1, 200 M relay X2, 400 M relay X2, 800 M relay X2, 1,600 M relay X2, 5,000 M relay X2, 110 M Hurdles X1, 400 M Hurdles X1, 3,000 M Steeple Chase X1, 4 X 100 M relay X2, 4 X 400 M relay X2, 20 k race walk X1, 50 K race walk X1, High Jump X1, Pole Vault X1, Long Jump X1, Triple Jump X1, Shot Put X1, Hammer Throw X1, Discus Throw X1, Javelin Throw X1, Decathlon X1

At times it will be just Eko or Indra (X1) competing. X2 will be events in which both Eko and Indra compete for the qualifying events unless another event is scheduled at the same time. If that does happen, it will be just one of the brothers. The fans in attendance are wondering about Aspyn and Susan. So much is discussed, but Eko and Indra mention nothing. Yet the questions have been non-stop from fans, the media, and even others competing with and against the Suparman twins. Everyone wants to know about Aspyn, Susan, and the babies soon to be born.

Yet the twins do remain silent each time they are asked a question about their wives and children. It just makes Eko, and Indra miss them that much more. With all of the events, they will have 2 or more times of competition to shrink the playing field of hopeful competitors seeking a chance to be Olympians this Summer. These games will take nearly a full week, including travel, to be over.

Eko will be competing in the single person track events:

100 M, 200 M, 400 M, 800 M, 1,500 M, 5,000 M, 10,000 M Marathon, 110 M Hurdles, 400 M Hurdles, 3,000 M Steeple Chase, and the Decathlon.

(M is Meters.)

Eko will compete in these 11 racing events, including the Decathlon.

Indra will be competing in the field events and two Race Walk Events

Pole Vault, Long Jump, Triple Jump, Shot Put, Hammer Throw, Discus Throw, Javelin Throw, Decathlon X1, and the Walking events: 20 k race walk and the 50 K race walk.

(K is Kilometers)

Indra will compete in these 10 Field and Walking Events.

Eko and Indra will teammates for the following Track Events:

100 M relay, 200 M relay, 400 M relay, 800 M relay, 1,600 M relay, 5,000 M relay

Eko, Indra, and two other Indonesian teammates will compete in the team races/relays - a total of 6 team races/relays. With 27 positions available for the single and team events, there could possibly be some type of schedule conflicts or issues. Yet, if anyone is capable of achieving this and performing excellently under pressure, it is both Eko and Indra.

For the team relay events, each race requires a total of 4 athletes. It was decided that Eko or Indra would be the first in these relay events, and the other brother would be the fourth, the last runner in the relays. That way, if any other country regains a lead, it would allow the Indonesian team to finish strong. After all, who can beat the Indonesians if one twin starts and the other twin crosses the finish line? Eko and Indra, even with their minds pre-occupied with all that is going on in their personal lives, are still very intelligent and have the desire to compete and do the best they are capable of doing.

As the games started, every person present and watching knew that they would see something that no one before them has ever witnessed. With the previous games, both current world records and Olympic records were being destroyed and replaced by Eko and Indra. After all, they both have running speeds of 364 miles per hour, faster than race cars. They're able to throw a baseball with perfect accuracy at a speed of 1,064 miles per hour.

The current records are not expected to be broken in every game they participate in; they are expected to be the best ever and possibly never to be broken again unless it is Eko and Indra breaking their own world records. That is all the talk unless it is about Aspyn and Susan, who are in the final weeks before the children are born. The media was just as interested in the babies as they were in Eko and Indra competing event after event.

The first day is starting, and as expected, the events are all overcrowded with people eager to watch either Eko or Indra compete. World and Olympic records are being shattered each and every time they are competing. Eko and Indra are missing their wives more and more as each and every moment passes. Yet, they push on, for they know that this is very important and must be done. They use that energy in the events they are involved in to push themselves to end the day.

As day two arrives, time seems to have slowed down for Eko and Indra, so every minute feels like a day. They have, for the first time, become homesick. Even those that are in attendance or watching on television or the live internet feeds can see that something is wrong with Eko and Indra. It is that obvious to everyone, even their teammates. When they are asked about their mood, they simply do not answer or say anything. The only people present at the games who actually know what is happening are Eko and Indra and also Michael and *"DJ"* Daniel Joe.

As day three is nearly ready to start, both Michael and *"DJ"* decide that it would be best for Eko and Indra to hear from Aspyn and Susan. Even though they would spend most of their free time calling each other, both Aspyn and Susan knew something was not right with their husbands.

Michael called Barbara and Idah and informed them of the situation. Barbara and Idah then went and told Aspyn and Susan. Both women wanted their husbands to be happy, now that everything is exactly as it should be. So Susan was now talking to Eko just as Aspyn was talking to Indra. Each woman made sure that her husband was better. That reassurance made a huge difference.

After talking to them, both men were again confident and ready to finish these events as they originally planned. With the final/last day of events coming to a close, the Suparman brothers once again achieved all the goals they set out for themselves during the Seoul, Korea qualifying events.

Chapter 16
Athens, Greece

The very last of the qualifying events were croquet and lacrosse, and they were to be held in Athens, Greece. This is the birthplace of the Olympic Games. The games were to start less than 30 hours from the end of the Korean events. So they all decided to go and finish up the qualifying for the croquet and lacrosse events, which would take a total of three and a half days to complete. Both wives and their doctors let Eko and Indra know that everything was perfectly fine, and the babies are in excellent health too.

Croquet was last an Olympic Event in 1900, and this is the first time since then that it has been re-introduced for the Summer Olympics. Croquet can be played by two, four, or six players. The object of the game is to hit your ball(s) through the course of six hoops in the right sequence in each direction and finish by hitting them against the center peg.

The side that completes the course first with both balls wins. These matches have three different classes with two, four, and six players. They were thus ideal for showing the world the different skill sets that Eko and Indra are capable of. Croquet is not a game where strength or speed matters. That's why these may be the most challenging events for the two brothers. Field lacrosse is a full-contact outdoor sport played with ten players on each team. The object of the game is to use a lacrosse stick or crosse to catch, carry, and pass a solid rubber ball in an effort to score by shooting the ball into the opponent's goal.

Each of these events will also be a round-robin of 6 teams. A total of 5 contests will be played in each round-robin. However, unlike some of the other team sports, they can play up to 3 games/matches in one day. If it were up to Eko and Indra, they would have played all the matches for both croquet and lacrosse in one day if they could. Yet the pre-determined schedule was made many months ago. Both Eko and Indra knew that if they were to win 4 of the 5 matches/contests in both events, the Indonesian teams would be advancing to the Summer Olympics.

It was determined by both brothers that if this occurred and the option is available, they would not participate in the final day of matches and let their Indonesian teammates see if they win without Eko and Indra. It is now the third day, and the fourth match of the croquet was won again. The Indonesian team was now 4-0 in all formats of the croquet team events. The last event today is the fourth lacrosse match. Eko and Indra decided to play offense for this game. During the first three matches, either Eko or Indra would play defense, and the other would play offense. However, during those matches, not a single opposing team was able to score a single point. In fact, none of those teams were in the offensive zone even once. This game was over in less than 20 minutes with both Eko and Indra in the offensive zone. The Indonesians were now qualified for the Summer Olympics, regardless of tomorrow's final matches in both croquet and lacrosse.

As soon as the final match is over, Eko and Indra immediately run to the Airfield, where both Michael and the *"DJ"* have been waiting. They all decided that they would leave once the final match was done and that Indonesia had achieved the last of the qualifying events of these games in Athens. Many of the fans in attendance thought that the twins were being rude and showing poor sportsmanship.

It was first seen as a sign of disrespect to leave. But once it was explained why they suddenly left as they did, all was forgiven by most people. The media, of course, decided to keep referring it negatively, especially since both Eko and Indra have been sheltered away from the media and news reporters. Either way, however, anyone took the news, it was their choice and Eko, and Indra respected that each and every person is allowed to think for themselves.

Chapter 17
March 16th

In the village, there are more people than ever before. All the villagers, as well as both Eko and Indra, are home along with Roger. Sheldon, Bill Bell, Ron Levi, and Dr. Vegarra are there as well. Also visiting are the British Royals, King William, Queen Kate, and their four children, along with Harry, Megan, and their son. Mr. Bill Gates and his wife, Mr. Phillip Knight and his CEO Doloris Thomas, along with the President of Indonesia and the President and Prime Minister of India, are also all there.

They and some personal security are all honored guests to be a part of the births of Eko and Indra's children. And, of course, both Aspyn's and Susan's parents are also present for this day everyone has been waiting for. After all, everyone here who is not part of the village has made friends here and also worked together in the efforts started by the success of *"The Perfect Season."* They have worked towards the goals of helping others in any part of the world to have a better life. The entire village, as well as the honored guests in attendance, have all been waiting for today, March 16th. No one even slept last night. Eko is with

Susan, and Indra is with Aspyn. Until now, it has been quiet. Then everyone hears Susan screaming, which is then followed by Aspyn screaming as well. Idah, Barbara, Kate, and Megan leave the remaining people waiting and go back to the two delivery rooms to check on Aspyn and Susan. That way, when the children are born, they can announce if they are boys or girls and let others know as well.

At 2:20 P.M., Aspyn gives birth to a healthy baby girl, and Megan leaves the room to announce this to everyone waiting. When Megan makes the announcement, everyone is cheering and celebrating.

At 2:21 P.M., Susan gives birth to a healthy baby girl as well. Queen Kate leaves the room to announce this to everyone who was still celebrating. Queen Kate enters the room and makes the announcement. Again, everyone is going wild, happy that two baby girls were born a minute apart to two different mothers.

At 2:22 P.M., Aspyn gives birth to a healthy baby boy. Idah leaves the room to announce this to everyone celebrating. As Idah enters the room where everyone is, they are all silent, for they know another Suparman child has been born. Idah then announces the news. They all are celebrating again that three of the four were born within a minute of each other. At 2:24 P.M., Susan gives birth to a healthy baby boy, and Barbara then leaves the room to announce this. Barbara enters the room and tells everyone, *"It's a boy, a healthy, beautiful boy."*

Everyone is hugging, kissing, cheering, and celebrating for it has happened. The twin brothers now have twins of their own, and all of them were born within five minutes of each other. Most importantly, all four children are perfectly healthy and rather large length-wise. Both Aspyn and Susan are also very happy and healthy. Everyone is so excited and happy about this special moment and will remember it for a long time.

Indra enters first, and he is carrying both his babies with pride and love. He makes sure each and every person, including even the security he doesn't know, gets a chance to see his two beautiful children. A few moments later, it is Eko's turn, and just like his brother Indra, Eko is carrying both of his children. He, too, is very proud and just as happy as Indra and makes sure each and every guest has a chance to see the children. Everyone attending must have taken a total of 10,000 pictures between them as each baby was introduced to all present, which is everyone in the entire village. All six of the doctors are now entering the room where everybody is.

Dr. Vegarra announces, *"All four babies are doing extremely well. Both Aspyn and Susan are also doing well, but we do want both Aspyn and Susan to have limited visitors, as both ladies need some rest."*

Everyone in the group thanks all the doctors for the part they played, and now it is time to celebrate. They are getting ready to celebrate this wonderful time that is somewhat historical. As mothers, only Queen Kate and Megan know what is ahead for Aspyn and Susan, and understand for what the children will be subjected to. Because of their experience, they are the first to speak and talk about what will soon happen.

Yes, many wonderful things happen when you are famous. However, there is also another side to fame, which isn't so wonderful. After both Queen Kate and Megan share stories of their previous experiences, Barbara and Idah begin to share looks of concern with each other.

Sheldon, knowing Barbara his entire life, instantly picks up on her facial expressions. The entire group has made a promise to make sure that these four children will not have to worry about evil people. They will be raised just as Eko and Indra were, but with modern conveniences that Eko and Indra didn't have as children. In this room are the most powerful people on the entire planet, with their wealth, influence, and experience. Their promise to protect these children will be honor-bound by the relationships they have created. All of the children here today – the babies that had just arrived, the children of King William and Queen Kate, Harry and Megan's son, Mr. and Mrs. Bill Gates' children, and the children of both Presidents and the Prime Minister – all of them will someday in the near future not just be associates, but rather lifelong friends who together can make greater improvements for everyone and keep the mission/goals that were recently started by Roger, Sheldon, Eko and Indra.

As the day passes quickly, the visitors outside have to leave group by group to carry on with their work and commitments. All have agreed that it will be up to the four parents, Eko, Susan, Indra, and Aspyn, to decide when they will share their story with the rest of the world. It will be on their terms as to when and with whom they will share the news in the outside world. One thing that everyone has agreed to is that all four children take after their fathers in one aspect. Whoever is changing the diapers will say it smells like Eko or Indra when they fart, meaning it was thunderous and just as stinky as it was loud. Even the mothers agreed, making Eko and Indra turn as red as the color of the Indonesian Flag.

Yet they always smiled when that comment was made and then warned the person that they would be fart-bombed by Eko or Indra for saying that. That instantly made the children cease saying that - well, at least while either Eko or Indra was within hearing distance. However, the older villagers who have known Eko and Indra since they first arrived were not fearful of the *"fart-bomb"* threat, for they have grown used to that smell.

Chapter 18
The village

Since the end of the qualifying events at Athens, Greece, both Eko and Indra have remained at home with their wives, newborn babies, and all the other villagers. But with Spring now nearly over, the Olympic Games were getting closer each and every passing day.

The Indonesian Olympic Committee Members had no idea where Eko and Indra were or lived. The President of Indonesia had it approved to make sure that Eko and Indra would be provided with the right tools to train, practice, and improve on the events they were not used to.

With Sheldon's help and approval, Barbara was responsible for picking up equipment at Jakarta, Indonesia, using one of Sheldon's jets. Then the jet would fly to Sydney, Australia, and then helicopter transferred to where Eko and Indra lived with the other villagers. It was during one of these transfers that someone, a pilot or a member transferring the items, somehow became aware of the four babies.

The person who leaked the information knew the children's names: Eko and Susan named their children

Doloris and Manual, who were named after Susan's parents. Indra and Aspyn named their children William and Doris after the names of Aspyn's parents. The leaker also was aware of how four children were born on March 16th within 5 minutes of each other.

The breaking story was being broadcast on every channel on television, every radio station, and every internet site. This made all four of the parents upset, but they knew this day was eventually going to happen. Still, they had wanted to make the announcement on their terms when they were ready. Now they are being forced by the leak.

When the news broke out, Barbara's phone rang non-stop. She received calls from the invited guests, and they all swore that it was not them who leaked or broke the promise they all made. Barbara knew that was true, for although it had been weeks, the only people who knew the names of the children were in the village, and the one and only outsider was Sheldon. It couldn't have been Aspyn or Susan's parents for they were still at the village and neither couple had even once used a phone or a computer. They were too busy taking care of their grandchildren. Each set of grandparents were having fun with both the twins and also the twins' cousins. It is a huge task to care for one baby, but everyone in the village was taking care of the four newborn babies.

Barbara knew it was not Sheldon; after all, Sheldon had always kept his silence when he made any promises to Barbara or anyone else that Barbara heard Sheldon made promises to.

When it was fully investigated, the investigators discovered that one of the additional security details had suddenly been paid a million dollars that had been posted to his personal bank account. When this person was questioned, he admitted that he was the one responsible for the leak, but he had only done this because of his wife's medical issues and really needed the money.

Sheldon was extremely upset about this. When they discovered that the leaker's wife was indeed in need of medical treatments, Sheldon decided not to have any criminal charges for what had happened. Sheldon and the others agreed to allow him freedom. A written agreement followed, where no one is to discuss this ever again, and of course, the leaker would resign. If the leaker doesn't follow the rules proscribed, it would be easy to prosecute for the crime. Once Eko and Indra learned of why this had happened, they were no longer upset. The only thing Eko said was, "Why didn't he ask us? We have doctors here and want no one here or anywhere else to suffer."

Yet what was done was done and couldn't be changed, for the news was out and creating more questions than answers. Now that the entire world knew of Doloris and Manual, and Doris and William, the media was all over this. They didn't know the location they were in yet, but it would be only a matter of time before that was leaked out the home they had in Australia was compromised.

Barbara, Sheldon, and Idah had a conference video call, and they decided that they would seek a new place for the day they happened to be discovered, and everybody comes to know where they actually live and reside. It was best to be prepared in advance, since the whole world is now interested in all of them: Eko, Aspyn, Indra, Susan, Doloris, Manual, Doris and William Suparman. After all, the Suparman family has grown from two to eight in less than a year. Yet the media only had a few pictures and the names of the two sets of twins. Idah made sure that when they move, the entire village will move together to wherever they will call home. With the Summer Olympics in Moscow ever so close to the beginning, a lot of things would need to be completed before the games started. Many people made offers, from Phillip from Nike, Bill

Gates, King William, and Queen Kate, to the President of Indonesia and the President and Prime Minister of India, to name a few that were close friends with Eko and Indra and their wives and fellow villagers.

All the resources came up with several different options, and this was the starting point. A new search was started for a new home. They had quite a few potential locations on islands near the Philippines, as well as options in the United States, England, Indonesia, and India. Any of these places had several options for the group to consider.

Once they were aware of these options, Idah called for a village meeting to discuss the same with each and every elder. As a group, they wanted what was best for each and every villager. Decisions like this must be agreed upon by the majority of the tribe and not by one or a limited group, for each and every person in the tribe were all treated with respect and being told the entire truth.

After this was brought up, many of the villagers asked Eko and Indra where they wished to live, for the villagers wanted to go where ever Eko and Indra wished. They wanted to be with the Twin Brothers, their wives, and of course, the four beautiful babies that were getting bigger by the day.

Eko and Indra had the same reply to every villager that spoke to them. They didn't care where they lived; they only cared that the entire village would all be together, wherever that may be. In many ways, both Eko and Indra believed they were the cause of these events and took full blame, even though it wasn't their fault and out of their control. What happened couldn't be stopped.

All the villagers had conversations with Aspyn and Susan. Knowing Eko and Indra as they did, they knew the twins were sad and believed it was their fault that they had to move again in less than a year.

Chapter 19
Searching

The villagers began searching for a new place to call home. Eko, Susan, baby Doloris, and her baby twin brother Manual, as well as Michael Dean, Idah, and a few other personal security, would be one of the two groups making this trip to inspect possible places they could call their next home.

The other group had Indra, Aspyn, baby Doris, and her baby twin brother William, as well as "DJ" Daniel Joe, Barbara, and a few more personal security too. By having two groups, they would be able to achieve twice as much, visiting more places in person.

Time was of the utmost importance and was slipping away; after all, the Summer Olympics are just a little over a month away from starting in Russia. Everyone wanted to have a place to call home before the games are to start. Imagine the Moscow Games start, and then their resources stretch thin. What if their home in Australia was discovered while the games are happening? Naturally, Eko and Indra would more than likely leave the games to be with the villagers. So they had to find a place before the games started. Each group travels to one destination after another, and the original list has not worked out for one reason or another. While they search, each and everyone involved stays in contact with those they know are true and real friends. They get told of places that they did not consider. People who have traveled to someplace and stayed and had a personal experience there would offer more suggestions.

Roger, who has been working all over the world, told Idah of places that he has been to. He suggests Abaco, the Bahamas, as the best of both worlds, thanks to the Bahamas' laidback beachcomber charm combined with "urban" conveniences. Marsh Harbour, the Bahamas' third-largest city, has a population of about 15,000, so urban is relative, but it offers convenient shopping and good schools. The surrounding cays are your playground. A short boat ride can make you feel like a castaway. And the locals that lived there are all as friendly as the villagers that Roger called family. This would be the one and only suggestion Roger gave to Idah.

Idah told the others, and they all agreed that the two groups should meet in the Bahamas then travel to Abaco. When both groups get together in the Bahamas, they see that it is quite peaceful. The villagers know of Eko, Indra, and their famous family but are very gracious, extremely friendly, and very down to Earth. Crime is non-existent in Abaco. As the group arrives at Abaco, they fall in love with the location and the residents that call Abaco home. The Abaco village elders are quite happy to meet the entire group and offer to show them around. When the elders learn that Eko and Indra's family and extended family are seeking a new private place to call home to live and raise their children, one of the elders said, "You have come to the right place. Your group is large and our village small, but there are plenty of areas nearby to make your own home."

The entire group is very happy to hear this proposal. The day is nearly at an end, and just like Idah's village, the villagers of Abaco invite the guests to come and eat, stay, and then see more of Abaco the next day. Indra and Eko waited until everyone fell asleep. The twin brothers sneak away from everyone and look for a possible spot - after all, they are the only two that can move as fast a bullet train. They can cover far more ground in a few minutes then the entire group can cover in a week.

Indra is waiting back on the camp for his brother Eko to return. Indra hears a "swoosh" and knows that Eko will be arriving in a matter of seconds. As Eko is now beside his brother, Indra says, "Did you find any place, Eko?"

Eko replied, "Possibly, little brother. What did you find? Any place you think would be a place for us to call home?"

"Yes, I did find a spot about 4 or 5 miles away," said Indra. "Would you like to see the place, Eko?"

Eko nods his head in approval, and Indra then takes the lead with Eko close behind.

Indra stops, and Eko is right beside him. Eko looks around and sees how there is freshwater near, plenty of room to build a village, and it is also close enough to the beach. They both look up into the sky, and the view reminds them of their original home back on the Island in Indonesia. The area is also far enough from the beach to keep this location away from prying eyes on a boat, or plane, or helicopter.

Eko then looks at his younger brother and smiles as he did the day the babies were born. Eko and Indra both agreed between themselves that this was so far the best place they had found or seen since they began this adventure. Yet, even though they were excited about this discovery, they decided to be quiet and allow everyone to sleep. When they are awake, they will tell the others and then take them to this location. They will have no vote in the move, but they will show them what they found and let the others make the decision if this is to be the next place they call home.

When the entire group awakens, they arrive at the spot with a few of the local elders. They are all are very happy with the location for it has everything they want and need: enough room, fresh water, and quiet, not to mention it is hidden and beautiful. It only takes a few minutes for everyone to agree; this is indeed perfect to call home, perfect to raise newborn babies, and with perfect weather. The elders also give their approval for them to call this place home.

After it is agreed that this is now where home is to be, Eko and Indra begin as only Eko and Indra are capable of and build one hut after another. Within an hour or so, they have made many huts for their tribe and family. The elders cannot believe how quick and efficient Eko and Indra are. One of the elders looks at Idah and tells her, "I cannot believe what they can do! Would Eko and Indra mind helping our village and some of the other villages when they move here?"

Idah smiled and replied, "Of course! Not only will Eko and Indra help, but our entire village, which is all family, will help. Eko and Indra will not be living here full time until the Olympic Games are completed, but when the games are done, they will usually be here most of the time, if not all the time and they are very helpful and enjoy helping others."

All the Elders are very happy with this news, and everyone in Idah's group is also extremely happy. Aspyn and Susan love this place; the weather is beautiful, the air is clean, and also the ocean is just a few hundred feet away. This is to be their future home, which is now nearly ready for all the villagers to have a place to call home.

Barbara then calls Sheldon to give him the news, and Idah is contacting the villagers also to give them the news. Sheldon now makes sure they can move as fast as a day or two, depending on when the villagers in Australia will be ready to travel. Idah is telling them to get ready for they are going to be leaving in a day or two, depending on how much time will be needed to get things packed and ready to ship for the big move.

Idah informs Barbara that the villagers can be ready in a matter of hours, and Barbara informs Sheldon the same. All the tribe members are also very happy and excited, and everyone is working together to make this happen as quickly as possible.

Chapter 20
Moscow

The villagers are now at the new location that is now home to them, and everyone is very happy. They are safe and secure as nobody knows where they are, except for a few that will honor their commitment to ensure the location is secret to the outside world.

The Summer Olympic Games begin in less than three days from now. Eko, Indra, Sheldon, Roger, Michael Dean, and "DJ" Daniel Joe are the only people that will be making this trip. Eko and Indra can return to their families and a new home with the rest of the family a little over 3 weeks after the games will be over.

Everyone is excited about Eko and Indra. They feel very comfortable leaving their wives and babies. After all, they are safe and healthy, as is the entire village. It is now time to participate in the Summer Olympics in Moscow, Russia. Eko and Indra's fellow Indonesian Olympian athletes have been in Moscow and are at the Olympic village, as are most of the Olympians from all over the world.

Quite a few of the Olympians in the pre-qualifying or qualifying events have seen Eko and Indra during those events. Others have actually competed against one or both of them. The Olympic International Committee and all the countries competing knew that unlike the previous Olympics, the security would have to be quite different and much stricter, especially with Eko and Indra being a huge part of these games.

One of the greatest things that do happen is the chance for all the Olympians living in the athletes-only Olympic village to get to know others from all over the world and develop new friendships that wouldn't occur otherwise. Eko and Indra were the most sought after athletes. All the other athletes were more interested in the newborn twins. As Eko and Indra would share with others pictures of the babies, everyone was surprised how tall they were for their age.

The Opening of the Games was stunning. Russia had put on quite a show. Now that the games are officially opened, the actual games are to start on Saturday, July 24th. The first events that will award medals today are Archery, Cycling Road, Fencing, Judo, Taekwondo, and Weightlifting. All 7 events will have winners accepting medals today. Eko will have 4 events, and Indra will have 5 events. This doesn't include round-robin events that will be the first round with additional rounds later. The round-robin events are Badminton, 3-versus-3 Basketball,

Football, Handball, Field Hockey, Rowing, Table Tennis "Ping Pong" and Tennis. Eight round-robin events are also starting today. Including the medal events as well as the round-robin events, either Eko and Indra or both would be in 15 events on the first, Opening Day of the Games.

If not for the agreement made many months ago, Eko and Indra couldn't have performed in all of these events today. With the scheduled changed to maximize the events, the only thing that may be necessary is that Eko, Indra, or both may have to leave an event early or join while it is already in progress. This would be acceptable for team events such as 3-versus-3 basketball, football, and field hockey events since they have teams with deeper rosters.

By the end of a long and successful day, they are glad to have worked things out as they did. All three of team events did indeed only have Eko or Indra for a limited amount of time. Eko showed up to the start of the 3-versus-3 Basketball game. After 8 minutes, the score was 172-0 in favor of the Indonesia Team. Indra played 8 minutes of the football game, and during the first 8 minutes, the score was 46-0 in favor of the Indonesia Football team. Both Eko and Indra played Field Hockey; Eko started and played for 7 minutes, and when Indra showed up, it gave Eko the chance to go to the next event. Indra played for four more minutes, giving the Indonesian team an unpassable score that would be impossible to beat with the remaining time.

On day one, Eko and Indra had between them both a total of 27 gold medals: 13 gold medals for Eko and 14 Gold Medals for Indra. In the weightlifting events, Eko competed in the unlimited weight class and Indra in the super heavyweight class. Both brothers won all 10 events each in their weight class. All the events were at the maximum weight that could, at the time, be used for any of the weightlifting styles. This time, both Eko and Indra did use both hands and did not disrespect any of the other weightlifters.

Indra and Eko broke all the Olympic and world records for every event they participated in, and these records would be impossible to beat unless it was Eko and Indra themselves in the future. The gold medal total for the Indonesians on day 1 was 27 Gold Medals. The President of Indonesia is the happiest person in Moscow since he wanted just one thing, and that was to win the most Gold Medals ever at any Olympic Event, Summer or Winter. The second thing is to win the football since he is now the Manager and Coach of the Indonesian Football Club.

It is now Sunday, July 25th, and today's team round-robin events are Badminton, 3-on-3 Basketball, 5-on-5 Basketball, football, gymnastics, and field hockey. The other round-robin events where only either Eko or Indra will compete are a canoe, kayak, handball, table tennis (Ping Pong), and tennis. They will have 6 team events in round-robin today and 23 individual/dual events. Canoe and kayak have 10 events each.

The events that both brothers will compete in different weight classes are boxing events. They possibly may also compete together in rowing, beach volleyball, as well as volleyball, if the schedule allows. (These are also round-robin events.) Yet, if the schedule has conflicts, only one brother will compete in these events. The one and only medal event today is the longer version of the Road Cycling. With 35 events today and only one medal event, today was to be an even busier day. Eko will be competing in the Long Distance Road Cycle. If Eko does win as expected, that will give each brother 14 Gold Medals each, and 28 overall Gold Medals for Indonesia.

All of the spectators, athletes, coaches, and media were able to have a full day of non-stop action. During team sports, they may play for as little as 4 or 5 minutes. The longest was 11 minutes in today's completed events. By the end of the day, Eko has tied with Indra for the most overall Gold Medals. Each brother now has 14 gold medals each, giving Indonesia 28 Gold Medals in just 2 days of Olympic Events.

Chapter 21
Record Broken

The overall Olympic record of 83 gold medals won by one country was in jeopardy. This had been achieved in 1980 during the Summer Olympics in Los Angeles by the United States. This record has lasted for 52 years, and by the end of today will likely be broken.

For the last 11 days, Eko and Indra have either alone, together or with another Indonesian teammate, won everything they have competed in. With only 4 more days until the 2032 Summer Games are over, most of the round-robin events are completed. Any remaining round-robin events are to determine the Gold Medal winner. There are still quite a few Gold Medals to be won and determined during these final 4 days of the Games.

The first final that is scheduled is Football. The Indonesian Team is facing the English team. Before the match between Indonesia and England, Eko and Indra were treated to a surprise that they were not aware of, for they have outside visitors visiting them in the Olympic village, even though security had a strict ban on non-athletes and non-coaches entering the heavily fortified and secured

Olympic village. Eko and Indra knew something was up for the other Olympians who were heard clapping and celebrating at the Olympic village, the athletes' home during the games.

It was none other than then King William, Queen Kate, Harry, Megan, and all their children, along with 8 other people. Being 8 feet 8 inches tall with eagle eyes, the twins instantly notice that is it the Royals with other people they can't quite make out. Both twins immediately reach the Royals, and as they see who the other eight people are, it makes them even happier.

It is Aspyn, Susan, Idah, and Barbara, and Doloris, Manual, Doris, and William, who have grown even taller despite being only a few months old. The entire Olympic village cheers. Eko and Indra are both very surprised and happy that their wives and children, the people they love the very most, are here with them. King William tells the twin brothers, "I hope you don't mind that I offered to have Aspyn, Susan, and the four children join us for today's match. Eko and Indra, I hope you may consider missing today's football match."

Harry then says, "You know my brother is joking, of course." Everyone laughs and giggles.

The other athletes all felt blessed that they were seeing not just the Royals but Eko and Indra's families too. Indra then asks the visitors, "Would everyone like to see where Eko and I stay at?"

Queen Kate said, "Of course, and we do hope to keep you both busy. After all, we are here to support you both, but we shall be supporting our team, England too."

Idah smiled and said, "Of course, just as Aspyn, Susan, Barbara, and I shall be supporting Eko and Indra and the Indonesian Club."

They arrive late for the football match in the second half. England is currently winning 5-0 against the Indonesian team. The President of Indonesia, who is also the Manager of the Indonesian Football team, is glad that Eko and Indra have arrived, finally. After all, the President's first goal is for Indonesia to win the most gold medals of all times during any Olympic games.

His other goal is to lead Indonesia to be the Olympic Winner in football. It certainly is his second most important and desired goal during these Olympic Games; after all, he is the Manager of the team, and if the team wins, then he as Manager will also be given a Gold Medal. The President was very angry before Eko and Indra arrived and asked them both, "Where have you been? We have a Gold Medal to win! By winning this Gold Medal, we can tie the all-time record of the United States."

Eko and Indra both looked into the skybox that seated Aspyn, Susan, their children, Idah, Barbara, King William, Queen Kate, Harry, Megan, and all the young royal children. They both point up to that skybox and inform the President that they were held back since they had to make sure that Aspyn, Susan, their children, and the others made it to their seats for today's Gold Medal Match.

The game is still going on during all this. The match has approximately 11 minutes left when they make the player change and have both Eko and Indra enter the field. Within two minutes, the score is now tied 5-5 with both Eko and Indra on the field. In the previous matches, they had shown they were capable of scoring 16 goals in less than a minute.

Nine minutes are remaining, and for the first time ever, Eko or Indra slow down, because they know they can go and score at any time. This creates time out from the Indonesian Team. As all the players on both teams leave the field for the time out, the President/Manager looks at Eko and Indra intensely. Red in the face from being upset, he says, "What is wrong with you, Eko and Indra? Why didn't you go and score goal after goal?"

Indra glanced at Eko and said, "Eko and I have decided that we will not score any more goals in this game."

The President nearly choked. "WHAT? WHAT DO YOU MEAN BY THAT?"

Eko stepped forward. "That is right, Mr. President. Indra and I will not score another goal. We want one of our other teammates to score too."

The President knew that if he upset the twin brothers, they may walk off or, even worse, quit. They are now two gold medals away from the overall record, his number one goal. He knows that without Eko and Indra, England would be nearly impossible to beat. The President then looked at both Eko and Indra, and at all the other teammates, whose facial expressions clearly support what Eko and Indra want to do.

He addressed the team. "Well, what is the plan, Eko, and Indra?"

Indra said, "We will play the game and defend, but we want the players to get into position to take a shot at the winning goal." Everyone on the Indonesian football club is cheering now, even the President.

As the match resumes play again, the English team has possession of the ball, which Eko and Indra had allowed. As they went to the mid-field to cross into the offensive side, Eko steals it legally and passes to Indra. Indra then looks for one of the other Indonesian teammates and sees one who is open. Indra passes the ball to the open forward, and the forward kicks the ball as the pass is arriving. The ball hits the inside of the back of the net for a goal!

The stadium erupts in cheers. The score is now 6 for Indonesia and 5 for England. With little time left in the match, Eko and Indra are true to their word. They stay back, so England has a chance. Indonesia has 6 Goals, and England has 5 Goals. Indonesia has won the football.

The match is over, and Indonesia has now tied with the United States for the Most Gold Medals at the Olympics. They have 84 gold medals for the 2032 Olympic games, with still more events to be completed.

When the events today end, Indonesia has 89 Gold Medals and is now the country to have the most gold medals during one Olympic Games. And still, we have three more days of events until these games are over.

EKO & INDRA

Chapter 22
August 8th

Today is the last day of the 2032 Summer Olympics in Moscow, Russia, an occasion which is now being called "The Greatest Olympics Ever" because of Eko and Indra. Not only did they have more viewers both live in person, but the television and internet feed also broke all records.

They have more fame and recognition than any actors, actresses, singers, musicians, world leaders, religious leaders, athletes, and the most powerful 1%. The 1% refers to the world's richest people, of whom Sheldon Winn is number 1 overall as the one and only trillionaire. Bill Gates and Phillip Knight are the others in the top three.

When the last of the final events were completed, both Eko and Indra each had won 64 Gold Medals each. Between the two brothers, that is 124 Gold Medals. They only shared when it was team events and quite often won Gold Medals in events that the other brother was competing in. Never did they ever have any direct competition against the other brother, as many had hoped and wished. Indonesia was now the all-time winner of Gold Medals in a Single Year for either the Summer or Winter Olympics.

The former record of 84 was now the second-highest, 36 Gold Medals behind the new and current Olympic winner, Indonesia, with 116 overall Gold Medals won by Eko or Indra. This made the President, all the Indonesian Olympic athletes, the whole of Indonesia, and the entire Asian Pacific very happy.

Without Eko and Indra, the three favorite countries for Gold Medal's favorites would have been the USA, Russia, and China. Before this year's games, they always were the top 3 favorites more often than not. Indonesia won all the events that Eko or Indra, or both, competed in. Sure, at times, they may have lost a tennis match or more, but when one of the twins showed up, it was over.

98.6% of the previous Olympic and World Record times/records were shattered for all the track and field events, all the swimming events, all the martial arts/boxing, and all the weightlifting events, just to name a few.

Before the ceremony ending and the games coming to a close, Eko and Indra agreed to be the last two Speakers for the final closing of the Summer Olympics. This is why everyone decided to wait until the very end of the games, whether they were present or viewing it on television or the internet. The world wanted to hear from both brothers; after all, they were when interviewed in the past, Susan, Eko's wife, was the one and only exclusive reporter. All the other reporters would have less than 20 seconds before the interview was over. Eko, being first-born, steps up to the podium near the Olympic Flame. As he approaches the podium, the entire stadium erupts and cheers him on. It takes more than a few minutes before everyone is again seated, and the crowd stops making noise.

Eko started his speech. "Greetings to everyone. First of all, I would like to thank my wife, Susan, who is the mother to our twins Doloris, the older one, and Manual, her younger twin. I would also like to thank My Brother Indra, his wife Aspyn, and their two twins. Believe it or not, they were all born on March 16th within five minutes of each other. My niece and nephew are named Doris and William.

Of course, I have a few others that I would like to thanks, as well. Roger Schafer, the first outsider and the Scout who discovered Indra and me. I also need to thank Idah, our mother. No, she isn't our mother by birth. She is better. She is not just Indra's and my mother; she is a mother to our entire tribe. Then there is Mr. Sheldon Winn. Sheldon, thank you. You are like my second father, after Roger.

I also would like to thank King William, his wife Queen Catherine, and all four of their children. I also want to thank Harry, Megan, and their son Archie Harrison, who prefers to be called Harrison." He looked directly into the camera. "Also to the President and Prime Minister of India. We will be back for the tigers.

Everyone who has supported me, Indra and our families, not just now but for our entire lives, thank you for your love and support, my family. Thank you also to all of the athletes, no matter where you come from. My Indonesian teammates, the fans both here at the games and also watching and supporting us from afar, thank you.

Russia," and here the crowd goes really crazy. Eko needs a few minutes for the noise to drop. "Yes, Russia, thank you on behalf of all the athletes, not just me and Indra. Thank you, International Olympic Committee, the Indonesian Olympic Committee and of course the President and also the Manager of our football club.

If I forgot to mention someone, please forgive me. Indra and I have been working on this since they asked us a few days ago. Speaking of Indra, let me introduce you. You all know him as an outstanding athlete. But I only know him as two things: my brother, my best friend, Indra."

The crowd jumps up from their seats. Everyone is clapping and cheering as loudly as they can. It takes a full five minutes for people to sit back in their chairs. As they become quiet, Indra begins to speak.

Indra started. "First of all, thank you, thank you all, each and everyone one. Now Eko did a fine job of thanking everyone. Since he covered that, this is how we want to close these games. This is one of the most important things to myself, my brother, our wives and everyone that he personally named in his speech, like Sheldon, Phillip Knight, Bill Gates, the Royal King and Queen with Harry and Megan, and of course Roger, Idah, our wives and Barbara. Together, all of us have been doing work all over the entire world. We have several missions, not just one.

Some of those missions are to ensure everyone everywhere has access to clean water to drink, food to eat, medicine and medical centers, schools to learn in, fields to play sports in like baseball fields, basketball courts and football fields. We are creating the structures for these. After all, look at what Baseball has done for us, Eko and myself, as well as my entire village and also all of Indonesia. Eko and I are not concerned with money or riches or power. We are more concerned with improving our entire world, and that is what we are doing.

No, I am not attempting to brag or boast. Rather I am telling you everything that we have been doing for the last several months. Rather I am speaking for all of us. We need your help too. No, we are not seeking donations, but if you wish to help, please do. We seek your help where you live. Do what you can. If you see someone homeless, give them water and food and let them know you care. If you see a person having a difficult time and can do something about it, do it. As they say at "NIKE," just do it.

Be kind to your parents, family, neighbors, friends, and strangers too. The world is a beautiful place, yet we can make it an even better paradise. What we are asking is something all of us can do and should do, even it is just a little.

I will again say thanks to everyone that Eko mentioned to our Russian hosts," here, again, the crowd goes wild. "Thank you, thank you all."

As the speech ends, the lights that have been shining on the podium begin to fade to darkness, and yet Indra is long gone. The crowd chatters away about what they just heard. The majority of the people present and watching do feel better instantly. They have been touched. Everyone cheers one last time as the Olympic Flame is now no longer burning.

The games are now officially over.

Chapter 23
Home

It has been a long journey for Eko, Indra, and everyone else. Once again, the entire village is home and all together. The villagers noticed how all four babies, Doloris, Manual, Doris, and William, had grown so quickly, and they say, "They grow as fast as their fathers. It won't be long before they are running."

All the other villagers who watched Eko and Indra grow up as children themselves agree that these four babies are growing quickly, and it won't be long until they are racing against everyone else, including their fathers. As they are preparing to sit by the fire and eat as they always do, people see some torch-bearing people come towards the group. It is the Elders and other villagers from the neighboring village.

As they arrive, they are all invited as guests of the homecoming celebrations that were about to begin. At first, the other tribal villagers declined the offer, for they didn't want to ruin a special event. But Idah made sure that they did stay; after all, they had more than enough food for everyone to get their fill. Michael Dean yelled out, "The more, the merrier!" And "DJ," Daniel Joe said, "I agree, so let us get this party started."

The other tribe, therefore, decided to stay and share with their neighbors. It is quite a festival evening, and as it nearing the end of the night and evening, the oldest of the elders from the other tribe is speaking with Idah and Barbara.

The Elder tells Idah and Barbara, "We did have some men while you were gone. They showed us pictures of Eko and Indra and asked if we had seen them or knew of anything."

Idah and Barbara's jaws both drop, and they shake their heads in disbelief. After all, they do not wish to move again, at least not so soon.

Barbara then looks at the elder and asks him, "What did you tell them?"

The Elder replied, "I told them that Eko and Indra were once here to see things with a large group, but what those things were, we didn't know. We told these visitors we heard you say this place wouldn't work, and that you were going to the next location. That was several weeks ago. We have not seen anyone since that day."

Idah said, "What happened when you said that? What did they do or say?"

The elder said, "They looked around at the others in their group and said, 'OK, scratch this place off. They have been here but are gone.' Then they left, and we did not see them again."

Barbara then goes to her hut/residence, and when she is back from the hut, she has a cell phone that she gives to the Elder. She tells him, as Idah still sits there, "Elder, if those men or any other men/women come through your village, simply use that phone. Dial 1 and it will call me, so we know people are out there looking for us."

The elder is puzzled as he holds the phone. Idah knows what his body language is saying without the elder saying a word. Idah looks at the elder and extends her hand for the phone. She said, "Let me show you, for when they gave me my first cell phone, I didn't know either. It is easy. See this button," and she pointed to 1 on the phone, "Just use your finger to push it, then put the phone like this to your ear and mouth. You'll hear ringing. Let me show you. Idah pushes the number 1 and places the phone near the Elder. He hears the ringing, which is followed by Barbara's phone ringing.

Barbara grabs her phone and then answers the call. Barbara then speaks, and the elder begins to laugh. He says, "I can hear Barbara here and on this device as well." Both women smile and nod their heads in agreement. Idah then shows the elder how to turn off the phone after the conversation. They practice this several more times, and after several attempts, the elder understands and also promises to do as they requested if anyone comes looking for Eko or Indra.

The night is getting even later. Most of the villagers from both tribes, after a belly full of food and a long day, are getting tired. Idah asks the other villagers to stay for the night, but the elders insist that they have done more than enough and that they need to get back to their village.

Eko and Indra whisper in Idah's ear. Idah looks at them, smiles, and nods her head. Eko then said, "Well, allow me and my brother to help you all get home if we can."

The elder said, "No need for that, since we know these trails and will be home in an hour or so. But thank you."

Indra grinned and said, "What if I told you that you could be home in a minute, and the others within a few minutes of that? Would you accept our help?"

The elder looked at his villagers and sees that they are very tired. He then agrees to the offer. Eko and Indra pick up one person each, and then they are gone, only to re-appear in a moment. The elder is stunned and looks at the twins. "Where are my villagers?"

Indra said, "They are home, and you can be next to see for yourself."

The Elder agrees as Indra picks him up, and Eko picks up another. Zoom! They are gone, already at the neighboring village. The people who have reached there are looking at one another now, and then again two more, and two more after that. Before you could count to 100, all the villagers are now home.

Eko and Indra said, "Goodbye," after the last of the tribe got home, but the younger villagers and small children all wanted to do that again. They were then told to go home and go to sleep, which they all did. Eko and Indra went back home to the village, and finally, they are all together at home. It has been a wonderful night of celebration. Everyone was happy. The only two who were not happy were Barbara and Idah.

It was a concern that strangers had been looking for their village. Barbara shared this with Sheldon. Sheldon, too, was concerned. He told Barbara to keep him posted, and he would get back to her later.

Eventually, the villagers who were not aware of this would learn of it, sooner rather than later. Sheldon couldn't help but think to himself how nice it would be for Eko and Indra to re-join the Conquistadors. Even though it was now August 11th, there was still plenty of baseball to be played as defending Champions. The Albuquerque Conquistadors only had 40 more games left of this season's regular-season games. With Eko and Indra committed to the Olympics, they had missed most of the regular baseball season, which Sheldon wasn't too thrilled about.

It was always assumed that Eko and Indra would rejoin the Baseball Team and help to defend the World Baseball Championship and give the New Mexico Baseball Team two championships in the first two years. The team had prepared for this a long time ago, despite having the lowest payroll in the previous season. They were able to pick up the free agents that they really wanted. Most of the new free agent players did not sign up for the Conquistadors for just the money. Many did it for a chance to be a World Champion. Others did for a chance to compete with Eko and Indra. Others, of course, did do it for the money.

The Team did keep a few of the first season players as well who were not Eko and Indra. Al Foster: Short Stop, Thomas Trujillo: Right Field, Angel Pineda: Second Base, and Chris Luttrel: Center Field. They were the only other baseball players from last season who were still on the team this season in year 2.

In the draft, they were able to get Austin Bell, the son of General Manager Bill Bell, who was now playing Center Field. They moved Chris Luttrel to Left Field. A solid catcher, Greg Miller, was also drafted - he has had a fine rookie season and had not missed a single game. General Manager Bill also loaded up on pitching to make a solid team.

However, at this time of the season, the record is 50 wins and 72 losses and could use a boost for the final 40 games of the season. Sheldon's ace had Eko and Indra with the team. No one will be looking for them. Plus, if people knew that Eko and Indra were playing baseball, the villagers would be safe and secure.

ROGER SCHAFER

Chapter 24
Reaction

Sheldon shared his thoughts with Barbara and Idah. "You know what would be best for Eko and Indra and everyone in the village? To have Eko and Indra come and finish this year's baseball season. We only have 40 games left and then the playoffs."

Idah shrugged. "I do not know Sheldon, for that would be Eko and Indra's decision. Besides, they have been gone for so long and now have babies. It would be their choice." Barbara nods her head and winks at Idah to show her approval.

Sheldon said, "Of course, Eko and Indra will make the decision, Idah. But I know that Aspyn and Susan's parents have been wanting them to visit. More importantly, by leaving the village, anyone that is NOW looking for Eko and Indra and also Aspyn, Susan, and the kids will no longer look for them, for they know exactly where they will be. Here, Playing baseball."

After a pause, Idah said, "Yes, that is a good idea, Sheldon, but it is still their decision."

Sheldon said, "Is Barbara with you right now, Idah?"

Idah said, "Yes, Sheldon, we have been on the speakerphone the whole time, you, Barbara, and I."

"Hello, Sheldon," said Barbara.

"Hello Barbara, I am glad you're listening too. If they choose to come to play baseball, we can make the entire village far more secure than it currently is. If they stay and we hire people to install the improved security, there is a high chance someone immediately leaks it. After all, the media paid a million dollars last time for just a few pictures and the names of the babies. Having the entire Suparman family out of site can make it easier for you and me to set up the best security and even perhaps change the landscape."

Barbara asked, "What do you mean by changing the landscape, Sheldon?"

Sheldon replied, "I was reviewing a new security method where they make it appear, for example, that there is a mountain that cannot be climbed over. Yet this mountain has a secret passage and keeps all others out. I was told that Mark Z at Facebook and even the Google owners are using this new security feature on some of their private islands. It is 99% effective."

Idah shook her head. "I don't understand Sheldon, but I trust you, and Barbara will explain it all to me later."

Barbara laughed. "Sheldon, you're a genius! Idah and I shall talk it over with Eko, Aspyn, Indra, and Susan and get back to you."

"OK," said Sheldon. "I will have a jet on the ground, waiting if you decide to do this."

Idah and Barbara walked towards Aspyn and Susan, who are watching their children play. Being able to walk, all four babies have started to learn about running and enjoy playing with each other as well as the children from their own and other tribes.

Aspyn and Susan said, "Hello," and Barbara and Idah greeted them in return. Susan said, "Ladies, I know you two well enough. What's on your mind?"

Idah said, "Barbara, I think you better tell them. It would be better since you understand."

Aspyn and Susan looked concerned.

"Yes, please tell us, Barbara," said Aspyn. "Is something wrong?"

Barbara said, "Last night, when the other village was here, the elder told me that a group of people was looking for Eko and Indra, and they even showed them pictures."

Aspyn immediately asked, "What did the elder or villagers tell them?"

Susan said, "They didn't tell them we are here?"

Barbara replied, "The elder told the people, that yes, they have seen us, but that we left and they heard from members of our tribe that this place wouldn't work. They did leave and have yet to return."

Idah took over. "I was with Barbara when the elder told us that last night. He also promised that neither he nor any of the other members of his tribe would tell anyone of us or Eko and Indra. But even so, I am still worried and concerned, not for Eko and Indra, but you two and those beautiful children."

Barbara agreed, and the four ladies silently went into thought together.

Eko and Indra arrived with some of the other villagers. They looked at each of their wives and could see that something was wrong. Eko asked, "What is going on? Something wrong?"

The ladies do not answer. They just look up. You can tell they are sad, upset, and disappointed.

Indra asked again, "What is wrong? Aspyn, tell me."

Susan then tells both Eko and Indra what happened.

Barbara then said, "Well, Sheldon does have a great idea."

Idah said, "Yes, I like Sheldon's idea more and more, Barbara."

Aspyn asked, "What is Sheldon's idea?"

Idah said, "You tell them, Barbara, please."

Barbara nods her head and then tells the group of Sheldon's plan to have the entire Suparman family, as well as Idah, if she wishes, to go and play baseball. "That way, if anyone is still looking for us, they will quit looking because they know where we will be: playing baseball. While we are doing that, Sheldon will have crews come down and install state of the art security and also some new security features which should make the entire village completely safe, 99% safer, according to Sheldon."

Idah chimed in. "Barbara, Sheldon also said that with the entire family gone, he would not have to worry about anything being leaked like before."

Barbara nodded. "Yes, Sheldon, and I agree that to have a lot of people down here will create attention. Plus, it may require a lot of people to install and do the things Sheldon wants. We can't possibly control leaks if any of those workers were to see Eko, Indra, Aspyn, Susan, or even the children, Idah or myself."

Susan said, "Well, I did promise my parents that I would visit and bring the children."

Aspyn agreed. "I know that feeling, Susan. Yes, maybe that would be best, not just for us, but for all of us in this family and in this tribe."

Eko and Indra agreed and got excited about playing baseball, which they still LOVE.

Chapter 25
Conquistadors

With only 40 games left in this season and a record of 50-72, it was important to finish strong. Now that Eko and Indra were coming to play, that certainly changed everything for the better for the Conquistadors. Before arriving at Kirkland Air Force base as they had during the entire last season, Head Coach Roger Chaves and General Manager Bill Bell had a meeting with Sheldon and Bernice.

Coach Chaves and G.M. Bill Bell thought this would be great and also keep the locker room from exploding, as all the attention will be on the twins. They would only need to pitch at certain times like every other game or every two or three games. Maybe Eko could be at Shortstop and Indra in Center Field."

Sheldon told them he would think about it, and they did have a good point on this. Bill said, "Sheldon when they get here, let them each pitch 2 games, so it gives our starters and bullpen a chance to rest their arms. Besides, Greg, our catcher, has played every game and every inning, and he could really use a break. Plus, this will give opposing teams a chance and make things interesting."

Sheldon is very surprised. "Are you saying that we lose on purpose, Bill?"

Bill said, "Absolutely NOT, but after watching them in the Olympics, I know that even if they don't pitch and catch, they can play the field. Do you think any player can even hit a home run with Eko or Indra playing center field? I think not. Even if they do, we still will have them hitting and scoring."

Coach Roger Chaves nodded his head in full agreement with what Bill is saying.

Sheldon said, "Well, Roger, you're the coach, and I see you nodding your head, so give me your thoughts and don't hold back."

Coach Chaves looks directly at Sheldon and responds, "Sheldon, we have a great locker room, two seasons in a row. Hell yeah, I wanna win! But what happens if Eko and Indra quit after this season? What we all have been building without them needs work, but we need most of these players we have to keep it going if we don't have Eko or Indra."

They all sit in silence for good twenty or so minutes. Sheldon then said, "OK, I have thought it over, as we all have. Yes, it will make it interesting, and yes, I agree we need to keep on building the team if we don't have Eko and Indra. Yes, we will do it!"

It is decided, and even though Eko and Indra are not aware, they will not be upset; rather, it will be just another challenge.

As they have made this decision, in walk Eko, Indra and Ron Levi, the tech guru. Ron said, "Hey, look who I ran into guys! And gals. Sorry Bernice, for calling you a guy."

Bernice snickers and says, "Hi guys, how are you doing, and how are those babies and my girls Barbara, Aspyn, and Susan doing?"

Indra said, "They are all doing good. How about you, Bernice? And Bill, Coach Chaves, and Sheldon, how are you doing?"

Eko said, "Bernice, all the ladies are doing well, including Idah." It is a somewhat unusual response, and Bernice and Sheldon both picked up on it. Sheldon gave Bernice a "YOU BETTER FIX THIS" look since Bernice had not inquired about Idah.

Bernice said, "Of course, I did mean to ask of Idah. I am very sorry, Eko. How is Idah?"

Eko replied more calmly now, "Idah is well. She and the others are here with us. They went to what will be home while we are Conquistadors playing baseball."

This filled Sheldon with joy and happiness. That was music to his ears.

Sheldon said, "Boys, or should I say, men, we are going to do some things differently this season, and we are going to share with the baseball world what we are doing."

Eko instantly asked, "What, we aren't playing baseball, Sheldon?"

Indra looks stunned; he has no words and is silent.

Bill quickly said, "No, you're going to play baseball, each and every game. Right, Coach Chaves? Feel free to tell them, Coach."

Coach Chaves asks the twins instead of telling them. After all, he is very wise and an excellent baseball coach. "Guys, how would you like to play in the field, like maybe one of you at Shortstop or second base and the other plays at, let's say, Center Field at times. What do you think about that?"

Eko or Indra don't verbally respond, for they are nodding their heads while giving each other high fives. It is very obvious they want to do this as well.

Bill said, "But you will still pitch every two or three games, and the other will catch since no one else can catch any of the pitches you throw."

Coach Chaves said, "Bill, you just sounded like that Abbott and Costello on "Who's On First" with a joke like that.

The entire room breaks out laughing, for even Eko and Indra had eventually understood that film and skit.

Coach Chaves said, "One more thing, guys. Do you care if you're team captains or not?"

Eko and Indra both said, "No, we just want to play baseball, and now we get to play in the field too!"

Coach Chaves said, "Well, we are going to have you each pitch in two-game each - the first four games back if you don't mind. Our pitchers need to have a rest and take a break."

"Anything you want, Coach, said both brothers at the same time.

Sheldon calls Jeff Ohm. "Jeff, you have the time to film an announcement?

Jeff is still very thankful for all Sheldon had done for him. He knows the most famous and requested cameraman, after all. Jeff was the former and only camera operator of Susan Vallelunga, better known now as Susan Suparman, wife to Eko and mother of twins.

Jeff had proven his work from his time as the one and only camera operator of Eko and Indra. He had even won awards for his work, and he knew this was something important.

Jeff reaches the stadium as quickly as he can. Sheldon, Bill, and the Attorney, John Sylvestri, are waiting for Jeff.

Jeff said, "Hey Sheldon, Bill, and John, what is up with you three?"

Sheldon replied, "Thanks for getting here on such short notice. I see you brought your camera."

Jeff grinned. "Sheldon, you told me to bring my camera."

Sheldon said, "Jeff, I would like you to film me making a statement, and wanted you to be the person shooting the footage."

Jeff said, "Of course Sheldon. You want to make that announcement with you sitting at the desk or somewhere else? I can set up the camera and lighting wherever you want."

Sheldon said, "The desk is fine, Jeff."

Jeff nodded. "Five minutes, and we will be ready to roll."

Jeff sets up the lights and audio. He runs a quick test on the camera and double checks. Jeff is now ready to roll, as he likes to say while filming. He looks at Sheldon and says, "Sheldon, we are going live in 3, 2, 1" and then points to Sheldon as an indicator that they are now filming.

Sheldon started. "Hello, everyone. This is Sheldon Winn, the proud owner of the Albuquerque Conquistadors. I am here to tell you that with the Summer Olympics in Russia completed, Eko and Indra are back and excited for the last part of the Season."

After a brief pause for a few moments, Sheldon continues. "But, and yes, I did say but, Eko and Indra will not be pitching and catching," Sheldon stops for a moment again and then says, "all season long that is." He laughed. "I got you all of you. They will each pitch, and of course, the other would be required to catch since no other human can even see their pitch except the other twin. I was 100% serious when I said they wouldn't be pitching and catching full time with our current team and this season's roster. We will continue with our pitching staff, and they will have a standard rotation once we get Eko and Indra in the lineup as an important part of our Conquistador Team."

"That means they will not pitch every game. Rather, after our first four games are done after Eko and Indra returning, they will be in the pitching rotation, and when they are not pitching, they have a desire to play the field. One will more than likely play a position in the infield, at Shortstop, for example, and the other will play in the outfield, such as Center Field."

There was a long pause, and then he continued.

"This will make the games far more interesting. We believe that we can be competitive, even though it is professional baseball, and winning is all that should matter. But we do this to make the game more popular and also…well, also to have fun. Have a good night. God Bless and Go, Conquistadors! See you at the next ball game."

The filming ends. Jeff, Sheldon, Bill, and John all review it. Sheldon is happy after reviewing the footage. As Jeff is breaking down the lights and other equipment, he looks at Sheldon and says, "Sheldon, are you for real about that?"

Sheldon grinned and said, "100% for real. Well, 90% for real, OK?"

They all laugh. Jeff said, "Well, Sheldon, I think it is cool, and it will be buzz material. You sure know how to operate and make things exciting."

Bernice, John, Bill look at Jeff and nod. Sheldon just chuckles. After Jeff has finished his task and is out of the room, Sheldon says, "Bernice, get this film to everyone in the media, pronto."

Bernice grabs the disc with the film footage and leaves Sheldon's office to get this announcement out to the media.

Chapter 26
Push

The push for the Conquistadors to have a chance to defend their World Championship was now in a far better position with Eko and Indra back. The baseball world, as well as the rest of the world, was thrilled at the announcement that Eko and Indra would be playing different positions at times and not just pitching and catching each and every game. Even more thrilled were the other 35 baseball team owners and the players on those clubs, for if it is true, at least, they have a chance to compete.

Ron Levi, the Tech Guru, was so excited to see Eko and Indra. Ron did notice how much more muscular the 20-year-old twins are now than from last season. They didn't grow any taller, yet at 8 feet 8 inches, they certainly were far more muscular than last season.

Ron whistled. "Wow, guys, you certainly are a lot bigger than when we first met. If you don't mind, let's go and see where your pitching speed and running speed are at."

By using Ron's technology, he wanted to confirm what the twins were capable of. Eko and Indra fully agreed, for it has been a long time since they stepped on the Conquistadors baseball field, and they were more than delighted to have some fun and as the tests ran. Indra said, "Yes, Ron, we are now twenty years old, and Barbara and the others have told us that all the Olympic training and events have made us stronger and faster."

Eko nods his head in agreement and then says, "But I am still the oldest."

Ron chuckles and then responds, "Yes, Eko, you're the oldest and will pitch first and then run first, too."

The two brothers are on the field in a split second, with Eko on the pitching mound and Indra catching. Neither of them changed or put on a baseball glove. After all, they didn't need gloves, but since it is part of the required equipment, they always wore a glove when on the field during games.

Eko's first pitch is at 1,172 miles per hour dead center, exactly where Indra set up the target to pitch to. Last season, Eko and Indra had a top speed average of 1,064 miles per hour. Clearly, they have increased the speed of the pitches. After fifty perfect pitches right-handed, Eko then proceeds to throw 50 pitches with his left arm. The same results come in - all fifty pitches are at 1,172 miles per hour and all right on target and dead center.

As Sheldon and Bill Bell have been watching this from Sheldon's office, they feel very happy, like children are on Christmas morning before unwrapping their Christmas presents. Eko and Indra were still able to pitch with amazing, uncanny, perfect pitches; those pitches are also even harder and faster than before.

Indra and Eko switch positions. It is Indra's turn to pitch, with Eko catching his pitches. Just like his older brother, Indra has the same results, 100 perfect pitches dead center, 50 pitches with the right arm, and 50 pitches with the left arm and all pitches at 1,172 miles per hour and dead center, perfect pitches.

Sheldon watched each and every moment of the twins doing this. He tells Bill. "Bill, you know I do have a little bit of regret for making a promise after watching this. But I did promise, and I will honor that promise."

Bill said, "Sheldon, we all watched the Olympics, and they have grown and improved since then. I don't know if it is because they are a year older or because of the training and the Olympics or both."

Sheldon said, "I would say both, and boy, do they look GREAT."

Bill said, "Think of it this way. When they are in the field, for example, the other team has a batter that hits what would be normal home runs, as high as Eko or Indra can jump. I bet you, Sheldon, that those hits, which normally would be a homer, will be robbed by the twins. Plus, they will be hitting and increasing our runs per game too."

Sheldon said, "Yes, I agree, and it will be exciting to see for the fans and everyone else watching."

Ron is now having Eko and Indra prepare for the base-running test. This test is when they are in the batter's box, and they leave it in order, touching each bag and the home plate last. Eko goes first, and as he knows this drill, he leaves the batter's box, touches first base rounds second base and touches it as well, rounds 3rd base and touches the base, and heads to home plate touching it as well. This is completed before a person can even blink their eyes.

The speed test also shows a vast improvement. Last season, they averaged 364 miles per hour running. Now it was at 411 miles per hour, and each brother did it 50 times in the left side of the batter's box and another 50 times each in the right side of the batter's box. It is confirmed; their running speed, just like their pitching speed, has improved from last season, and they were even faster than when they competed last season or even in the Olympics.

Ron is giggling and happy.

Eko said, "Ron, we are glad to see you so happy, but tell me what is making you this happy?"

Ron looked at both brothers. "Because my math was correct, and it has been confirmed just now."

Eko and Indra really do not understand what Ron said, so they just respond with a smile. Ron's cell phone rings, and it is Bill Bell. Sheldon and Bill have been watching the entire time, and after seeing the results, Bill tells Ron on the phone, "Ron, do me a favor. Keep both of the guys on the field, and we are going to have Coach Chavez, who right now is leaving the equipment room, have Eko and Indra do some fielding warm-ups, drills, and try a few things."

Ron said, "You bet, Bill."

Coach Chavez arrived with a couple of the others from the club in the golf cart. Sheldon and Bill have also left the office, and all of them are on the field. Sheldon said, "Eko, Indra, guys, if you don't mind, how about Eko goes out to

Center Field and Indra go over to Shortstop? We are going to have Coach Ron, and the other coach hit some balls to you and do some fielding practice drills."

Both of them are happy to do this and are in their positions in less than a second. They have two Coaches hitting fielding practice at the same time. One is hitting to Eko, and the other is hitting to Indra. Eko, in the outfield, has caught each and every hit. Bill looks over at the Coach hitting the baseballs to Eko and gives a thumbs-up. The thumbs-up was a sign that Eko and Indra didn't know about, but it means that it is time to hit baseballs that would be home runs.

Eko is not aware of this. He is in position, and the first time they do this, he leaps nearly 30 feet in the air and catches the baseball. That baseball would have been a home run if it were a game, yet Eko just jumped 30 feet and grabbed the baseball with no problem. In baseball, when something like this happens, it is referred to as "being robbed." That's because the outfielder robbed the person that hit this, and instead of the hit being a home run, it is caught for an out.

Indra at Shortstop has been outstanding. He too even robs hits that would have been a home run time after time.

Eko, too, had the same results, hit after hit. Sheldon is glowing with joy, as are Bill and Coach Chaves. The brothers switch positions, and the results are the same. They're perfectly doing things that only Eko and Indra are capable of doing.

When it is over, Eko and Indra tell everyone how much fun they had. They loved doing this. Sheldon was not as worried about making this decision now and knows that it will keep a lot of interest and make things exciting for all fans. The final push of the regular season with 40 games was a push in the right direction, even with the new changes and challenges for Eko and Indra.

Chapter 27
Playoffs

It is game 122 for the Conquistadors today. For Eko and Indra, it is game 1 of 2032 since last year. The stadium is packed. There have been media requests from worldwide to broadcast this event, the official return of Eko and Indra as baseball players for the Conquistadors. It was just like last year on the Opening Day of the season all over again, with all the excitement.

Eko was to pitch this game, and that would require Indra to catch today. For the rest of the team, today's game is number 123 of 162 games in the regular season. The Conquistador pitching staff and the rookie Catcher Greg Miller needed a few games to rest and recover for the last part of the season.

All the teammates were excited. Many new players were on the team this season, and they worked hard without Eko and Indra around. Eko and Indra knew this season was different, and after being Olympians, they learned things that they hadn't realize before. As Olympians, they learned how important it is for the entire team to be involved. They welcomed this season's changes, as did the fans and spectators. Eko only needed his normal 81 pitches, which were all strikes; it was impossible for anyone to even swing at his pitches – well, anyone not named Eko or Indra Suparman. Game two with Eko and Indra involved Indra pitching and Eko catching. Indra, like his brother, had also only required a minimum of 81 pitches. The results were the same for game 3 and game 4, in which Eko and Indra have played since they returned.

The Conquistadors now have a record of 54 wins and 72 losses. For the rest of August and most of September's games, Eko and Indra did not pitch or catch; rather, they were playing Centerfield or Shortstop. Sure, they would rotate as they always have done in the past, but one would play Centerfield and the other Shortstop. They robbed many hitters hundreds of times and made plays that were impossible for any other person. They were a pitcher's best friend. The overall pitching stats were now highly improved after their return, and this showed in all the stats of pitching: ERA "Earned Run Averages," wins, etc.

Sheldon was even surprised by this, and never once during this stretch of games did he even ask or suggest to have Eko and Indra pitch and catch. The regular season has ended, and now the Conquistadors' final regular-season record is 90 wins and 72 losses. They did make the playoffs; they were not the National League West Conference Champions, yet they did make it as a Wild Card and were in the playoffs. In the playoffs, the Conquistadors had to win the first game without Eko and Indra. It all went as expected, but then the unexpected happened. All four children had suddenly become ill, and the worried fathers left the team, for they had to go and be with their wives and children. It wasn't anything serious; the flu bug had hit Doloris, Manual, Doris, and William. But since they had never been sick a day of their young lives, getting the flu for the first time was something that worries Susan, Eko, Aspyn, and Indra.

The great news is that the Conquistadors won even without Eko and Indra. They did win the first game of the Wild Card, even though it took 8 additional innings to have a game 1 winner in the first round of this year's post-season games. As Eko and Indra returned for game 2, they were so proud and happy about how well the Conquistadors played in Game 1. The Conquistadors won Games 2, 3, and 4 to sweep the opposition and go on to the finals of the National League.

The National League finals were again a sweep by the Conquistadors. Even this deep in, Eko and Indra did not pitch or catch; they were now full-time field players. The games were certainly more entertaining. The world record for television and internet ratings even broke last year's records, which was important; after all, to lose viewership means that fans are not interested. Yet that wasn't the case, with all the friends that Eko and Indra have made. Eko and Indra playing positions instead of pitching and catching have created even more fans. All Conquistador merchandise is completely sold out as well.

The National League Champions and the Defending World Champions were now ready to begin the first game of the Final Championship versus the American Champion. Since the American League Champion had a better overall record, they will have the home-field advantage. The first two games would be played at the American Teams stadium. Games 3, 4, and 5 would be played at the Conquistadors. Yet everyone knew this would be a four-game sweep, or so they assumed.

The first three games of the best of seven were all won by the Conquistadors, and it is now game 4. If they win this, the Conquistadors will be back to back World Champions. The game was in Albuquerque at the Conquistadors stadium, yet the field was very slippery for it had been raining – it had been more of a downpour. Despite the advances made by Ron's computers and technology, human officials were still a part of the game for events like this; they would determine if the game is to be played or postponed due to the heavy downpour which finally has stopped. It is now confirmed that Game 4 will go forward and happen. The teams take to the field; Eko is playing Centerfield, and Indra is at Shortstop for today's game. The American team is first to bat, hit and pitch. They swing at the pitch, and it is blasted. Eko runs, but he slips and cannot jump as he normally has thousands of times since playing. The slippery field causes Eko to twist his ankle, and he is hurt, as he lands awkwardly on the field.

The hit was a home run, and Eko, for the first time since his return, did not rob the hitter, and the American League Champions had a score of 1-0 in their favor with just one pitch. Eko was still curling in pain. Indra was by Eko's side when it happened. The other outfielders and the rest of the team were now surrounding Eko as well. The stadium was silent, even as the batter crossed home plate. He and his team were concerned for Eko, yet they were also celebrating because, for the 1st time in this series, they had a lead.

Dr. Vegarra, the Conquistadors Team Doctor, and Ron were next to arrive in a golf cart. After several more minutes, Indra is seen helping Eko stand up, but everyone sees that Eko cannot stand on both feet for his left lower leg wasn't even touching the ground. Eko, with Indra's help, was loaded into the trailer that was attached to the golf cart. As Eko takes off his baseball cap, he looks into the crowd and waves to them; this is a sign that he is ok. Everyone cheers, including the American Team; after all, no one wants to see anyone get hurt or injured. This was the first time that either brother had an injury. The stadium was silent, which had never happened in a single game that Eko or Indra have ever played in. As Eko, Ron, and Dr. Vegarra are leaving the field in the cart and trailer, all the fans and all the players and coaches are giving Eko a standing ovation. A brief time out is called, and as all the players on each side go to their benches, it is quite obvious to each and every player and coach on the Conquistadors bench that Indra is rather upset. Coach Chaves then makes a move and moves Indra to Centerfield and has Al Foster go and play shortstop.

Before they leave for the field, Coach Chaves tells his team, "Men, listen, with the field being in the condition it is, I don't want anyone of you to do something that could hurt you. Indra that means you as well."

They all understand, and as they are leaving, tears begin to form in Indra's eyes. By the end of the top half of the 1st inning, the American League was winning 3-0. It was time for the Conquistadors to bat, and with Eko out of the game, Indra will be hitting first. Yet, the American team's pitcher gives Indra an intentional walk. The American team knows as soon as the catcher begins to make the throwback to the pitcher after ball 4 is called, Indra will have scored by stealing all the bases using his speed. And Indra did just that; he scored a run before the catcher could even throw the back to the pitcher on the mound. The score was now 1 for the Conquistadors and 3 for the American team. The game was a loss; this was the first team loss for Conquistadors after they had Eko and Indra play. The score ended up being 6-3; Indra scored all three runs with intentional walks, and his teammates were unable to help or get any runs, for the American team's pitcher pitched the best game of his life.

This created quite a stir, for no one had thought this would happen. The team and fans were waiting for news on Eko's playability in game five. They found out it was a high ankle twist/sprain, one of the worse twisted ankles that takes time to heal and would require medical clearance before Eko was allowed to play.

A few hours before game 5, Eko was officially ruled out of today's game, and even possibly games 6 and 7 if those games are needed to determine a World Champion. Sheldon was very concerned as he wanted Eko to play. Yet as the doctor stated, "If he does play, this injury could cause even more damage and may end his career entirely."

So the team doctor didn't give his clearance, and Eko was to miss a game because of his injury. The team is now moments away from the start of today's game five. The Conquistadors are all fired up. As a team, they have dedicated today's game to Eko. Eko is present and is on crutches. He feels sad that he can't help his teammates, yet when they tell Eko they will win today for him, he is very happy. As they leave the locker room and go down the ramp, they are glad that the field is dry without any rain. They are ready for Game 5.

Not only did the team play excellent, by the end of the 6th inning, but they were also leading 16-0. Indra had only scored 4 times, and each time he was walked. Coach Chaves made a change in the top of the 7th inning, and he actually pulled Indra and had him replaced. As soon as Sheldon knew this, he immediately called Coach Chaves and said: "What are you doing?"

Coach Chaves said, "We are going to win this game, and if we don't, fire me."

Sheldon then shook his head in disbelief and just hung the phone.

On the 9th inning, the Conquistadors were winning 19-4. The American Team did score three more runs to give a final score of Conquistadors 19-7. But they did it! The Conquistadors were the back-to-back champions and the first-ever expansion team to win the World Championship in the first two seasons, EVER. At the end of the game, everyone is celebrating, even Eko, with crutches. The Conquistadors are all together, including the wives and children of the players. Susan, Aspyn, and babies Doloris, Manual, Doris and William, Idah, Roger, Barbara, and everyone else in the Conquistadors' organization are all celebrating.

Barbara goes over to where Sheldon is. Their eyes meet. They smile at each other and give a hug to one another. Barbara whispers in Sheldon's ear, "Sheldon, thank you. When Idah spoke to the villagers, they said that you promised to improve security, and with the new features, there haven't been any issues. Thank you, Sheldon."

Sheldon whispers, "Barbara, thank you. I hope you will be coming back to Albuquerque too. I miss you."

Barbara said, "I miss you as well, Sheldon, yet my home is with them, and I hope you understand."

Sheldon just smiles, and Barbara knows that Sheldon understands that she will be not returning to Albuquerque. Barbara is now part of that family with the Tribe and villagers.

Chapter 28
Recovered

It has been six weeks since the final baseball game was played. Eko, Indra, and their wives and children have been back home with their village family for the last five and a half weeks. Eko has fully recovered, and life has been quiet, and the security is working better than expected.

Eko looks at his brother and says, "Brother, I feel better than I have in a long time. Doctor Vegarra said everything is healed and well..."

Indra said, "Well, what, brother?"

Eko said, "Well, I think it is time for you and me and the entire tribe to go to the happiest place in the world Disney Land, and then to India where the Tigers are."

Indra was excited. "That is an excellent idea! And we can bring our families and everyone else in our village to Disneyland and India."

Indra goes to were Barbara and Idah are sitting. As usual, they are watching over the children playing.

Idah asked, "What has you so excited, Indra?"

Indra then tells both women what Eko proposed. The ladies see how happy Indra is, and they agree. After all, it will be something that the entire village can do after a long year. Barbara then dials on her cell phone and calls Sheldon.

Sheldon answers his cell phone. "Hello Barbara, how is my best friend doing?"

Barbara said, "Well, hello to you, Sheldon. I have a favor to ask."

Sheldon said, "Anything for you, Barbara."

Barbara said, "Well, remember last year how we had that night at Disneyland?

Sheldon said, "Well, of course. That was wonderful. Do you want me to set up something for Eko and Indra with them?"

Barbara said, "Yes, please, Sheldon, but make it for the entire village here, and also for the neighboring village too."

In the background, Idah, loud enough for Sheldon to hear, says, "Yes, for all of them and us, but make sure you also have the teammates, their families and also King

William, Queen Kate, their children, as well as Harry, Megan and Harrison.

Sheldon then responded, "Barbara, ask Idah if I too am invited?"

Barbara laughs and then asks Idah, "Sheldon wants to know if he can come too."

Idah laughs as well. "Of course, Sheldon is part of our family, that silly man."

They are all laughing. After an hour or two passes, Barbara's phone rings. It is from Sheldon.

Barbara answers her phone, "Hello Sheldon, I bet you're calling..."

Sheldon doesn't wait for Barbara to finish her sentence. "Yes, Barbara, it is all arranged, and even the Royals will be attending. I will have three jets for both tribes, and then we all will meet in Disneyland. We have the entire park for 24 full hours this time."

Barbara said, "Thank you, Sheldon. We will see you soon."

Barbara then goes and informs Idah. Idah says to her family, "Everyone, we must go to our friends in the tribe near us, for I have something to tell you and them, and I want to make this announcement at the same time."

Everyone agrees; after all, Idah is the Mother and the leader, and then all of them make their way to the elder's village, the people who are their friends and protect the secret of Eko and Indra.

Normally when Eko and Indra are home in the village, they would usually run their tribe over one by one. Yet now, they are all walking as a group, and Idah is leading the way.

As the other villagers see Idah and her tribe, they get up together to greet their neighbors. Idah and the other tribe elder are having a private discussion. Once they are done speaking privately, the elder announces, "Everyone gather close for Idah has a surprise for us all." As both tribes move as close to Idah, Idah looks to see that everyone is paying attention. Satisfied that they are, Idah says, "Everyone, we are inviting you to join us, to celebrate."

Many cheers are heard, for they all love to celebrate. One of the elders is heard asking, "What are we celebrating?"

Idah said, "I want your tribe and my tribe to go on a trip in a plane to the happiest place in the World."

Eko and Indra jump up and down in joy, yelling, "Disneyland, Disneyland! It is indeed the happiest place on Earth."

The villagers of Eko and Indra's tribe were aware of the stories Eko and Indra shared from their one and only visit to Disneyland. After the other village is informed about Disneyland, it is 100% agreed.

Later that afternoon, they, both tribes head to the airfield where Sheldon has three jets waiting to take them all to Disneyland. As they arrive in California, they are all transferred to Disneyland. It is now midnight.

For the next 24 hours, both tribes are all having a wonderful time. Doloris, Manual, Doris, and William love Disneyland, which makes the parents very happy. After their day at Disneyland, they all are exhausted and loading up to transfer back to the airport.

Sheldon is with Eko, Indra, and the Royals. He asks the group in his bus, "Did everyone have a great time?"

They all cheer. Eko says, "Sheldon, can we all go to one more place before we go home?"

Sheldon said, "Sure, where do you want to go, Eko, India, perhaps where the Tigers live?"

Indra said, "YES to India and the TigersI know, for I want it too, and we promised."

Sheldon asked, "Promised?"

Eko then tells Sheldon about the time they were in India and went to where tigers lived and promised the President and Prime Minister of India that they would be back with their family. Harry, King William's brother, tells the group, "I know what you're talking about, Eko and Indra. We love that place, too, and I am good friends with the Prime Minister and President."

Sheldon said, "OK, who wants to go to India to see the Tigers?"

Everyone on that plane responds, "YES!"

Sheldon then lets the pilots know that they will be going to India. Queen Katherine has spoken to the Prime Minister of India, and all is good to go. As the groups arrive at the airfield, there are now four jets, the three that Sheldon owns and also the one which brought over by the Royals from England on the Journey to Disneyland. Eko, Susan, baby Doloris, baby Manual, Indra, and Aspyn, baby Doris, baby William, Sheldon, Idah, and Barbara are on the flight to India and flying with the Royals on their jet.

During the trip to India from California, the men and women all decide that to make this a fun trip, they would invite several others.

Those others were Roger, who has been working very hard with the foundation, Phillip Knight and his most trusted Doloris Thomas, and Bill Gates and his wife. They all together have been making the world a better place, and still, many things must be done. Together, they will discuss what needs to be the next step and also make sure the changes they have made are still in full operation.

As the four jets arrive in India, Phillip, Doloris Thomas, Bill Gates, and his wife are waiting with the President and Prime Minister of India. It has been a long flight, and knowing the custom of Idah, they are informed that they will be going to have a feast, as well as a chance to rest, shower, and sleep. Tomorrow, they will all be going to the tiger reserves in India.

Eko said, "Tiger reserves? I thought they had only one tiger reserve?"

The Prime Minister said, "No, Eko, we have many tiger reserves. On your last trip, we only had time to see one of the tiger reserves, and we hope to show you several other tiger reserves."

Indra said, "Tell Eko and me about these other tiger reserves, please."

The Indian President said, "The best Tiger reserves in India are:

#1. The Bandhavgarh National Park, Madhya Pradesh.

#2. Ranthambore National Park, Rajasthan.

#3. Pench Tiger Reserve, Maharashtra – Madhya Pradesh Border.

#4. Kanha Tiger Reserve, Madhya Pradesh.

#5. Tadoba- Andhari Tiger Reserve, Maharashtra.

#6. Jim Corbett National Park, Uttarakhand.

The Prime Minister then says, "Eko and Indra, when you were here, we went to the Jim Corbett National Park. We hope to share the others with you, your families, and all the guests you have brought."

During their time at the reserves, they learn about how few tigers are left in the world, along with many other species that are endangered. The children are very upset and sad about this. Barbara said, "We need to do something about this."

Susan said, "Yes, yes, we do, and we need the people here to work together for endangered animals. This group can do a lot of great things."

Barbara said, "We should also address the pet issue, the dogs and cats that have been abandoned and are in shelters too."

Everyone agrees and decides that they will do what they can. They all decided to again make a promise and partnership for the endangered species worldwide, and also have something for pet over-population or pets that were no longer part of a family and in a shelter.

After two full weeks of learning about the tiger, all the guests are told of the number of animals that are endangered: elephants, tigers, lions, rhinos, whales, and many others. They realized that the time for fun is over; it is time to do something for the endangered animals and also the pets that have been abandoned as well. It is time to make the world an even better place for these endangered species, so their children's children will be able to see and know of these beautiful animals before they are extinct.

They will have two organizations effective immediately. They will also be protectors and work to have a better solution to make animals stop being extinct and endangered. Roger then says, "You know I am going to need more help. I fully agree with this, but I am so busy with everything else we have and are doing."

Sheldon responds, "Well, I know now what Ron Levi will be working on next - a way and means to protect these endangered animals from poachers, and we are going to even use satellites and technology to make this happen."

Roger asks Sheldon, "What's next, Sheldon?"

Sheldon replies, "Well, I was hoping to have a New Mexico Soccer team."

King William, hearing this, says, "I hope not."

King William and Harry are both laughing at King William's response, as is everyone who heard it. Eko and Indra go to the group and ask them all, "What is so funny?"

Roger tells them, and Eko and Indra laugh, then look at Harry and his brother William. Indra says, "Well, Sheldon, if we do play football, we promised the Royals we would be in the English League."

Sheldon doesn't respond - he rolls his eyes and knows it is best to be quiet. Megan and Queen Kate are speaking to each other. Megan asks the Queen, "What do you think will be Eko and Indra's next adventure?" Aspyn, Indra's wife, has an answer, which she shares with everyone. "The Next Adventure will be the Winter Olympics in 2036!!!"

It is now time for everyone to go home. This adventure is closing. Life is wonderful. Life is great, and most importantly, life is what you make it. So make it the best and live the best you can; after all, each and everyone can make life beautiful and should.

Until the next adventure of Eko and Indra!

ROGER SCHAFER